See A Side of Bridlington

by

Bridlington Library Writers' Group

ISBN 978-1-291-62903-3

Copyright © Bridlington Library Writers' Group 2013

All rights reserved, including the right to reproduce this book, or portions thereof in any form. No part of this text may be reproduced, transmitted, downloaded, decompiled, reverse engineered or stored in any form or introduced into any information storage and retrieval system, in any form or by any means, whether electronic or mechanical without the express written permission of the author.

This is a work of fiction. Names and characters are the product of the author's imagination and any resemblance to any persons, living or dead is entirely coincidental.

Published By

25 South Back Lane
Bridlington
www.lodgebooks.co.uk

Foreword

I often said to my husband, 'You're a great writer but you don't get on with it.' This applies in part to this Anthology; the Writers are great writers and *have* got on with it! Full of original material, well-constructed and pleasurable reading. Why not take a look!

Christina Butler
Patron of the Bridlington Library Writers' Group

Acknowledgements

Before this Anthology is unleashed upon the general public, and flies off the shelves, we must pay tribute to our intrepid shepherdess, Sarah Hutchinson.

Sarah is our leader and the founder of Bridlington Library Writers' Group. Somehow, she has managed to keep her flock penned in the fold for enough meetings to complete this Anthology of members' work. And that takes some doing!

Thanks also to our local publishers, Lodge Books: Susan for her high editing standards and Andy for his excellent design work.

Bridlington
by Michaela Goodale-Truelove

It is said that people make a house a home. They are also responsible for putting the heart into our villages, towns and cities. They set a tone, a unique psyche into a community, often by the jobs they do, the hardships they have faced or even the weather. Whatever it is, it adds a rich diversity across our land which can change and alter within just a few miles.

Bridlington, the coastal town where I live with its many characters and personalities, is just such a place. Times and our economy have played their part in recent years, making the Bridlington of today a very different place to the one of my childhood. I grew up in a town with a busy, fishing and manufacturing industry and numerous individual businesses before the arrival of the large supermarkets. A town jam packed with holiday makers, where hoards of local boys waited at the bus and railway stations with their home made barrows ready to collect the visitors' suitcases.

Times may change and our economy may grow or weaken but one thing remains constant, our geography. We live in a town where the sea meets rich fertile land, a land deep in history. An area of outstanding natural beauty, where hardy, tight knit families have survived and made their living for generations by farming crops or fishing. Throughout history people have chosen to settle in our sheltered bay to make a life for themselves. Historical evidence shows us, instead of dividing our societies these immigrants have been absorbed, adding a richness to our culture in terms of shaping our language, sensibilities and architecture.

Archaeologists have discovered some 3,000 years of mankind's habitation in and along our coastline. Bronze Age settlers established long track ways known as High Street and

Wold Gate. Numerous Iron Age earthworks and enclosures have been excavated. We have been invaded by the Romans who established a series of signal stations along the coast as protection from warring bands of Picts, Saxons and other "barbarians". Greek geographer Ptolemy described Bridlington Bay, at the time occupied by the Parisi tribe, as "Safe-haven Bay".

As for the origins of the name Bridlington there is no single definitive answer. Different cultures and the evolving nature of our language have produced many variations originating from the Anglo Saxon "Berhtel's farmstead" and the Norse word for smooth water, "berlingr", giving us Brillintona, Berlington, Breddelington, later Burlington, before finally settling on Bridlington, which incidentally happens to be the only one in the world. Many older residents today often refer to themselves as "Bollington Jackdaws".

We are called Bretlinton in the Doomsday Book. William the Conqueror gave our lands to Gilbert de Gant, nephew of King Stephen, in 1072 and it was his son Walter who founded our Augustinian Priory in 1113. A mere fraction remains of the 12th century Priory and Bayle as a result of Henry VIII's dissolution of the monasteries. What a story this masterpiece and remarkable survivor could tell of the past 900 years.

King Henry V visited in 1415 to give thanks to the town for our victory at the Battle of Agincourt. I wonder how many Bridlington long bowmen sailed across the sea and into battle for King and country.

By the mid 13th century until the early 16th century the settlement at Bridlington harbour was given the name Castleburn, meaning "fortifications by the stream".

During the civil war Queen Henrietta Maria took refuge in the town. Leaving behind her gloves (now in the possession of the Bayle museum) she also gave a ring to a family who aided her survival.

In 1779 residents bore witness to the Battle of Flamborough Head, a unique sea battle the like of which has never been seen in our British waters before or after.

It is said for many years there existed two parts to the town, two settlements, the Old Town and the Quay. Many believe it was the arrival of the railway in the 19th century which finally pulled the two settlements together. An old lady once told me about fights among young men if either side strayed into the other's territory. She spoke of the railway line on Quay Road as the dividing line.

Early in the last century fighting was to come for the whole of the country in the shape of two world wars. Many who left to serve their country were never to return to their beautiful corner of England. The town was also bombed and locals were to lose their lives.

Over the last century my parents and grandparents have witnessed advances in medical research allowing us to live longer, healthier lives, a welfare state and education for all, creating opportunities for my generation which they could only dream of. We are by no means living in a perfect world. However, I believe we need to open our eyes and cherish the natural bounty mother nature provides us with. We would do well to mind the American Indian saying: "We don't inherit the Earth from our Ancestors, we borrow it from our children", this powerful message to look after our world is an important sentiment in protecting the natural resources and beauty of every village, town and city, including those of Bridlington, for future generations to come.

Our Bridlington
by Joan Saxby

Bridlington is soon to be
Regenerated, refurbished, then you'll see
Our beautiful town on the English east coast
Yorkshire's pride, of which we can boast.

Tourists will come from far and wide
To visit this town of which we'll have pride
To enjoy its clean sea and pristine sands
They'll come on ships from far off lands.

There's Flamborough cliffs and a lighthouse too
Lovely walks and lots to do.
We have the historic Priory Church
So come along and do your search.

Bridlington
by Mark Cunningham

Beaches that are flat and clean
Restaurants cater for all cuisine
Idyllic places to sit and relax
Donkey rides thrill kids to the max
Leisure World for swimmers and muscles to tone
Ice Cream parlours serving a delicious cone
Not forgetting coffee shops serving tea with a scone
Go to Sewerby Hall and enjoy a tour
Take a scenic trip on a land train on the south shore
Or on the cliff top
Not forgetting we have delicious flavoured ROCK!

Watching The People Flow
by Trev Haymer

The bent-propellor flight of an approaching bird
Crosses the sun-path to my new, gull-tattooed seat
Where I'm watching the people flow, but there is
Nowhere to perch here in Brid Town's flocked street.

Where a gaggle of giggling, black-eyed girls surge along,
Nested half globes quivering, white as spring lambs
They're bleating into ear-clamped phones –
'She says like... then he says like... she goes, she goes...'
Then they are gone.

Followed by designer-dressed babies riding designer prams
Driven by designer mums who pilot designer cars
And dwell in designer homes. Next there'll be gaudy but neat
Designer coffins blessed by designer priests.

There stands a wet-nosed Big Issue girl,
She's glum-faced and stamping cold toes,
She's like a log that's splitting the flow
So I wait for the drip
To fall from the perch of her nose lip.

Here's a busker in full flow,
Wearing a tatty jacket and dickie-bow,
He's murdering a song I used to know
Singing: 'I got me no place ter go.'

A man slides by clutching a bike-less mudguard
That writhes like some demented black snake.
A pensioner creaks past in a shabby fawn mac,
It's topped with a brown tweed deerstalker hat –
He's shaking two charity bags and dragging

A small dog with upraised leg that's lagging.
A black-hatted Holy man sweeps past with silent children
hard-by his frocked coat
Now here scurries a woman sporting a bright red frock –
Blue lips, blue shoes, blue nails and high purple hair,
She simply just doesn't care.

Here's a little girl waving a hand,
She's throwing baskets of smiles around,
She's happy to still be on this land
But sadly she's broken, wheelchair bound.

Laughing students slither by – fresh faces buried
In the moist warmth of Cornish pasties,
Their hot meal for the day,
They glance at wreathes perched on the War Memorial
Some bright red – some dead like the carved names
Of men that people know – men no longer in the flow.

A canyon of buildings speckled with bird dung –
But there's no trout here in this fast flowing river
Of souls teeming with shoals of the young,
The old, the black, the white all bumping along
These boiling rapids of humanity –
All chords in the rhythm of the street –
All children swept into the flow
Of this stained and troubled planet's woe.

Friday Afternoon Shopping?
by Michael Perry

All I could make out was mumbling as I got ready to go for a window shopping afternoon that Friday. Well it was a nice sunny day, I'd nothing much to do and fancied a stroll round Bridlington, now lunch was out of the way. Michael was upstairs, probably on the computer.

A louder mumble followed by a clear, "Dear," came from upstairs. "Yes," I called from the bottom of the stairs. "I'm looking for my cricket gear, can't find it, love," he called from our bedroom.

"Try the wardrobe in the spare bedroom," I replied, and went back to the list I'd started in the kitchen of the few bits I needed from Boyes in the town. Just as I put the list in my bag over my arm he walked into the kitchen, with his cricket whites in one hand and shirt and pullover in the other.

"It's the old boys versus the young ones cricket match tomorrow," he said. "Bill's just rung and needs me as some of the others are away on holiday or past playing now."

"Tomorrow," I repeated, looking at the creased shirt and the trousers still showing grass stains and muddy marks on them from when they were last used.

"Yes that's right," he replied, dropping them on the floor in front of the washing machine. "Can't let the old team down can I? Must check on my boots and bat out in the shed," he said as he exited the back door.

Why is it we're too proud to let our men go out looking untidy or in clothes in need of a wash and press when they won't put them out for wash after they've been used? Well you can't just wash two or three things can you? So it's upstairs to bring down the washing basket to make up a worthwhile load. So much for shopping; I didn't need to wash that day but at least I could wash and dry a full load. The weather was great for drying and as I pegged out the lineful Michael, sitting outside the shed oiling his bat, said he was glad he'd managed to get me in time to wash his cricket gear with the other things I'd had to wash and, had I put the kettle on.

As I took him his pot of tea later, he sat there eyes half closed enjoying the warm sunshine. "Just waiting for the first coat of linseed oil to soak into the bat," he said dipping a ginger snap into his cup of tea. I never saw him touch his bat again, I was too busy taking in the dry washing and ironing his things for the important cricket match.

Bill and Sally called to take us to Sewerby Cricket Club on Saturday, after a rushed lunchtime cuppa and sandwich. The men, sitting in the shade of the pavilion veranda, looked the part in their clean pressed whites watching the match. Sally and I were volunteered to help make the sandwiches and put out the rest of the picnic items as well as prepare teas and coffees for the interval.

The cricket whites went back into the wardrobe, in the spare room. They'll stay there untouched again until next year. As it turned out the men weren't needed to play in the team at all. We must remember to put next year's match date in our diaries. But next year Sally and I have said we're going shopping before Bill rings up.

The Song Of The Sea
by Audrey Bemrose

Come with me on the shore
On a crisp clear day in spring,
Taste the salt upon your lips,
Fly your kite on the end of a string,
Turn your face to the wind,
Watch the ceaseless waves roll in,
And list to the song of the sea
As the ceaseless waves roll in.

Sit with me on the beach
Where happy children play,
Paddling in foam tipped blue
In the brightness of summer's day.
Relax in a holiday mood,
Watch the boats bobbing out in the bay,
Hear the soothing song of the sea,
Round the boats bobbing out in the bay.

Work with me on the sea,
Man the boats, haul the catch, mend the nets,
Gaze with awe at the wonders of nature,
Myriad colours as autumn sun sets.
Sense the power of the sea,
As we turn once again for the shore,
Feel the rhythm of the song of the sea
As we turn once again for the shore.

Pray with me on the cliffs
As the lifeboat men challenge the storm,
Because in the teeth of a winter's day
The sea has a different form.
It mercilessly pounds at the headland
Aggressively vicious to see,
Claiming lives and eroding our coastline
Aggressively vicious to see.

The song of the sea in crescendo
Has a beat with an evil power,
Turning the hearts of men to stone
When they hear it in danger's hour,
But the song of the sea has a haunting tune
That ensnares those hearts of men,
And a mystic refrain brings them back to the sea
Again, and again, and again.

Gypsey Race
by Patricia Susan Dixon MacArthur

Beck of our childhood adventures
Exploration of the unknown
Pools and puddles, pipes and tunnels
Leading down to its harbour home.

In summer green leafy, glade-like
Autumn, carpet strewn golden leaf
Winter, ice-cold bare-wood barren
Spring snowdrops unfurl from beneath.

Wild mallard's splashing-crash startles
Bank rats scurry frantically
Angry blackbird has a chunter
seeking food in the hedge, he's free.

What pleasure we hear in the trickle
of this waterway flowing along
This beck shares our dreams and nightmares
through the whole of our lives all along.

The Best Side of the Ocean
by Julia Oldham

"Yankee doodle dandy," plays the ice cream van.
We never get to hear the end of the tune.
The train rattles from side to side as it breaks into the countryside. You know when it is approaching the station because you hear a slower rhythm from the rocking carriages.
The aroma of hot fish and chips curling out from the café doors is like an addictive perfume.
The squeals of shock and delight from young children as they rush into the cold waves for the first time of the summer season.
The lusciousness of ice cream that drips down the cornet faster than you can slurp it up.
The bright lights in the amusement arcades where the electronic noises of the machines vie with the groans of another pound lost.
A walk along the promenade in winter, wrapped up against the biting wind and enjoying the heavy thud of the waves on the desolate sands.
Remember the closing scene in Pretty Woman, where the man walks across the road, saying, "This is Hollywood!"
This town ain't Hollywood . IT'S BRIDLINGTON!!

The Body in the Library
by Anne Mullender

Amanda walked down South Marine Drive past the newly refurbished block of luxury apartments, all with their blue-railinged balconies and bright tubs of flowers. The sea lashed fiercely against the sea wall sending frothy white cascades over the footpath along the South Promenade. As she walked past the Spa Theatre she noticed a man stuffing a very large packet into the postbox outside South Marine Drive Post Office. Wonder who that is? she thought. Just being nosy, she told herself. He kept glancing over his shoulder as though he expected someone to be watching him. His brown hair in a ponytail, he was dressed in tatty blue jeans with slashed knees and a dirty white tee shirt. Amanda noticed there were tattoos on both his arms.

Quickly she went on her way, for it was now just past eight thirty, past the Blue Lobster with its "Early Birds" poster advertising two meals for the price of one from 5 pm to 7 pm, round the corner past the newsagent's and the cheap clothing shops, continuing up Bridge Street. As she waited for the *little green man* to show and allow her to cross the road she felt in a very happy mood. Tomorrow, Ian was taking her out to the Flaneburg at Flamborough for a special meal for her birthday. She was looking forward to it and she wondered if this was going to be the night he would propose to her. She had felt they were a couple from the very beginning and she knew he was *the one* for her. Feeling elated, she hurried across to the back entrance of the Library. Going in she could hear Jack, the Caretaker, singing loudly from the basement. She looked at her watch. It was eight forty-five. As she ran down the stairs she rummaged about in her large carpetbag, which along with her packed lunch and a spare pair of shoes plus all the usual paraphernalia carried by young women, contained the key to her locker.

"Morning, Jack. Am I the first?"

"Morning, love. Yes, you're the first all right."

Amanda stuffed her belongings in her locker, changed her shoes and combed her long hair.

"Right then, I'd better make a start!"

"I've put all the post and newspapers on the counter, love."

"Thanks, Jack. I'll see to them."

Amanda went through the "In" door. The sun was now shining through the high windows down into the General Library. The familiar smell of books rather reminded her with a pang of nostalgia of her school days when, first thing in the morning on entering the classroom, there was that very pervasive smell of books and wood and an expectant atmosphere of the day's forthcoming events. She felt a quick rush of excitement as she surveyed the scene. Such a wealth of literature and knowledge stood on the shelves lining the walls - just waiting to be discovered and treasured.

There was the usual mound of post and newspapers on the counter and Amanda sorted through the post and put it on the Enquiry Desk in readiness for Louise, the Administrator, when she arrived. Picking up the bundle of newspapers and magazines she noticed that lots of compact discs were strewn about on the floor. The display stand offering local bus timetables and items of local interest had been knocked over. Thinking this was odd, instead of going into the kitchen to put on the kettle for the first morning cup of coffee for the other members of staff, who would be arriving any moment now, she ran through the "Out" door into the corridor.

"Jack! Jack!" she shouted to the Caretaker.

"Were you calling?" he answered down in the basement.

"Can you come up, please?"

"Just look in here, Jack. It's an awful mess."

"Blimey, love, what's been going on? I never noticed all that when I came through before."

"I think we ought to look upstairs. Will you come with me, please?"

Jayne, another Librarian, was just coming in through the

door.

"Hi, Amanda, have you put the kettle on?"

"Jayne, thank goodness you've come. There are lots of CDs on the floor in there," she said, pointing into the main room, "and someone has knocked over the bus timetable display stand, too. Jack and I are just going to have a look upstairs."

Jack and the two young women cautiously climbed the stairs and he slowly pushed open the Reference Library door. At first they could not see anything. The sunlight was very bright. Then they noticed that yesterday's newspapers were strewn about the carpet and a couple of chairs were on their sides on the floor.

"What a mess, who could have done this?"

"Looks as though we've had an intruder, love."

As their eyes became accustomed to the brightness they noticed that there was a dark stain on the floor. Amanda drew in her breath quickly.

"I think that looks like blood," she mumbled. "There's something sticking out behind the counter."

It was a foot in a dirty trainer and as they went round to investigate they saw the body of a man lying on the floor in a pool of blood.

"My God!" exclaimed Jayne.

Just then a voice was heard downstairs.

"Where is everybody?"

"Louise, up here!" shrieked Amanda. The girls heard her running upstairs.

"What's wrong? You sound frightened." The Administrator came in breathing hard. "Now, what's the matter?"

The girls pointed to the trainer-clad foot.

"There's a body!" they exclaimed in unison.

"Well, now, let's have a look," Louise said patiently, not taking in immediately the urgency of the situation.

As she looked over the counter and saw the lifeless body lying there she whistled in disbelief.

"Don't touch anything! Have you called the Police?"

Amanda shook her head. She walked dazedly over to the telephone and picked up the receiver. There was no dialling tone. She shook the receiver, but it was clear that the line was dead.

"Right," said Louise. "Okay, Amanda, go across to the Halifax and ask if you can ring the Police from there!"

Amanda ran down the stairs and out into the street. She gulped in the fresh air. Her legs felt as though they did not belong to her and she realised she felt quite sick. She managed to run across to the Halifax and push open the heavy glass door. Several of the staff were at their places behind the counter waiting for the first customers of the day. She called out to Helen, the Branch Manager, who was sitting at her desk in the office.

"Please, Helen, can I use your phone? Something awful has happened!   There's a body in the Library!"

Helen's face was a picture of consternation. Quickly she handed Amanda the phone. She dialled 999.

"Emergency - which service do you require?"

"Police!" Amanda shouted into the receiver.

"I am connecting you," said the voice.

"Oh, hurry, hurry, please, Police!" cried Amanda almost in tears.

After what seemed like an eternity: "Police Emergency Services, Newcastle. How can I help you?"

"Newcastle?" shrieked Amanda. "I wanted Bridlington Police!"

"Please state your name and address," the voice said patiently.

"Amanda Raper, 32 Meadowfield Road, Bridlington," she uttered. "There's a body in the Library where I work! Help me, please."

"Yes, madam we will put you through."

Soon a voice said, "Bridlington Police Station, P C Dixon. What can I do for you?"

"Oh, it's Amanda Raper. I work at the Library in King Street and I've found the dead body of a man in our Reference Library upstairs. Please, help. There's an awful mess!" exclaimed Amanda.

"Right, miss, what is your name and address?"

Amanda could not believe she had to go through all that again.

"I've just given my name and address."

"That was to Newcastle Police, miss. I need your name and address and the telephone number from where you are calling!"

Amanda obliged.

"Right, miss, we'll send someone along straight away. Don't touch anything!"

Thanking him, Amanda put the phone down and began to tell Helen what had happened. Helen was intrigued.

"Who do you think it is?"

"I really don't know, but he looks awful," said Amanda. "Do you want to come and see for yourself, Helen?"

"No fear," said Helen emphatically, "tell me everything at lunchtime. We can go and sit on the harbour wall."

"Right," said Amanda, "I'd better get back."

Amanda hurried back across the pedestrianised street not really noticing anyone or anything. She was feeling a bit better now but her heart was thumping with trepidation as she went in through the Library door.

"They're coming," she called out as she climbed the stairs. "They said we shouldn't touch anything. Do you think it would matter if we had a cup of coffee? I feel sick."

"That's a jolly good idea," said Louise. "Let's go downstairs."

Jayne took Amanda's hand and slowly guided her out of the Reference Library. "Come on, Amanda, I don't think they will have been in the kitchen and I think we could all use a cup of coffee!"

"Right you are, girls, that is a very good idea," said the Caretaker.

They all went downstairs. Jayne had just filled the kettle and plugged it in when two men came in through the back door.

"Good morning, we are Police officers," said the dark-haired one showing them his authorization. "I'm Detective Inspector McMinn and this is Sergeant Collins."

"Oh, thank goodness you've come!" cried Amanda. "The body is upstairs in the Reference Library and there's a lot of blood."

"I think he's been stabbed," said Louise. "These two girls and the Caretaker found him."

"I see," said the fair one. "About what time did you find him?"

"It was just nine o'clock - just after Jayne arrived," said Amanda.

"We'll have a look and then I shall need a full statement from you both. Collins, tell the people waiting at the front door there's an emergency and the Library will be closed this morning."

"Very good, sir." Collins went outside.

Quickly, the others went upstairs. When they went into the Reference Library, D I McMinn walked over to the body lying behind the counter and rolled the man over. He seemed more annoyed than anything, thought Amanda.

"That's torn it," he said. "They've done for young Harper, that's for sure!"

"Do you know him, Inspector?" asked Jayne.

"Yes, my dear, I'm afraid I do. Shall we say he was helping us with some enquiries," replied McMinn.

Sergeant Collins sighed. "This is going to put the cat among the pigeons, sir, and no mistake," he said.

"Well, no point in crying over spilt milk!" uttered D I McMinn. "We shall just have to get on with it."

He looked at the body and started to go through the pockets of the black leather bomber jacket the man was wearing.

"Ah!" he exclaimed. "What's this?" and he pulled out a crumpled envelope which had the words *Panamanian Flag* on it and the figures *10.30.*

"What can that mean, sir?" asked the Sergeant.

"Well, Collins, Panamanian flag must refer to the flag being flown on a ship, would you think?" replied D I McMinn.

He pulled himself together and told everyone to go downstairs and he would send for a Police Photographer and a Pathologist who would examine the body to see if there were any more clues and Forensics to come and look for fingerprints and other evidence. Collins went out to the Police car and made the necessary arrangements.

While they were having coffee, which Amanda prepared, the Inspector asked the girls to make statements, to be taken by Sergeant Collins. Afterwards he told them, "I will get someone to come and see to your telephones." By this time Mr Cooper, the Chief Librarian had appeared and had heard, with astonishment, the statements the two girls made to D I McMinn. Mr Cooper was then taken upstairs to see for himself the gory sight and fainted on the spot! Sergeant Collins helped to bring him round and asked Amanda to give him some strong black coffee to revive him.

"I suggest we all take the day off," Mr Cooper said. "There's nothing we can do here but be in the way, don't you think so, Inspector?"

"Absolutely," replied D I McMinn, "but first we must have a set of all your fingerprints. Then you can all go home. By tomorrow we shall have everything tidied up for you. You will have to put a notice outside telling people you're closed."

The Pathologist and a team from Forensics arrived and after their fingerprints were taken Amanda told Jayne that she was meeting Helen, from the Halifax, for lunch and they were going to eat their sandwiches on the harbour wall, did she want to join them?

Jayne said, "No thanks, I've had enough. I'm going home. See you tomorrow!"

Amanda picked up her carpetbag and set off across the street to seek out Helen and see if she was free to go for lunch. The sun by this time was beating down on their heads as the two girls walked up to the harbour and thankfully Amanda sat down and took a long cool drink from her tin of Tango. Excitedly, she told Helen of all the morning's happenings, dramatically emphasising everything as she told her story. Helen listened with bated breath.

"Wow! Fancy that happening just across the road from us! Why do you think they killed him, Amanda?"

"I expect we shall find that out, soon enough, Helen."

As they sat on the harbour wall, they noticed out in Bridlington Bay that there was a huge ship lying at anchor just outside the harbour. A young man Amanda knew came up to them. Part of his job was to supervise the unloading of the boxes of fish from the fishing vessels when they came into the harbour and to take down official details for one of the main firms who owned the boats. The fish was then loaded on to lorries and transported to be frozen and packaged at their factory in Hull.

"I was working on the fish dock and heard the Coastguard telling the Harbour Master that a German cruise liner was coming in about 8.30 am to anchor off Bridlington. The passengers were to go to York for the day," he told them. "About 100 of the German guests were to be ferried ashore on the cruiser's own red emergency launch and then be taken by coach to York for a shopping trip. Some of the other guests had asked to spend the day in Bridlington."

Showing off to the two girls, he pointedly remarked that the cruise liner was flying a *Panamanian Flag.* Amanda remembered then that the note, which the Inspector had found had said Panamanian Flag and *10.30* on it.

"I must tell Inspector McMinn," she said feeling important.

Amanda and Helen thanked the young man, Robert, for his interesting information and since Helen had to be back at work, Amanda accompanied her part of the way. As they passed the New Inn, a white-fronted pub with flower baskets framing the doorway, they noticed three men, deep in conversation outside. Judging from their beautifully tailored light trousers, immaculate sports shirts and soft leather shoes and guttural accents, Amanda decided that two of the men must be some of the German visitors from the cruise ship. Amanda backtracked to the newsagent's next door to the pub and nosily tried to listen to what they were saying. They were talking to a third man who was wearing a black suit, a black collarless shirt and black suede shoes. She thought he would have looked a bit like Al Capone if he had been wearing a black hat too. Her sense of humour must be returning, she mused. Listening to them she was sure she heard the *man in black* say *In die hohe Strasse in der alte Stadt.* In her schoolgirl German she thought she heard him say something about Barclays Bank as the men started to walk round the corner.

Amanda walked determinedly back to the Library and asked Sergeant Collins if she could speak to Inspector McMinn.

"I think it would be best if you were to ring him from home, miss, he's at the Station - the number is 672222."

"Thanks, Sergeant, I'll do that then," agreed Amanda, and she set off to walk the half mile up to her home in Meadowfield Road. Near to the bus stop on the Harbour Top she paused to talk to Mr Nicholls, who was standing on the pavement against his landau and his beautiful Palomino, Henry.

"Hello, Mr Nicholls," called Amanda. "It's a beautiful day, isn't it? Can I give Henry a Polo?"

"Of course you can, lass. Are you going home early?"

"Yes, we've had an exhausting morning. I found a dead body in the Reference Library. Oh, it was awful, Mr Nicholls," she said.

She stroked Henry's nose and he nuzzled her hand as she usually had one of his favourite mints for him. She opened her hand at last and he delicately took the Polo from her.

"Good boy," she said.

Patting him on his neck she said goodbye to Henry and to Mr Nicholls and set off towards home. As she walked up South Marine Drive she noticed that the sea was now gently rippling on the South Beach and she thought it was a pity that she really didn't have time to walk up the beach and paddle in the softly lapping surf.

When she arrived home her mother was in the front garden gathering flowers for an arrangement she was going to put in the hall. Amanda kissed her mother on the cheek.

"I have to make an important telephone call, Mum. If you put the kettle on for a cup of tea I've got something to tell you."

Feeling full of importance, Amanda picked up the phone and dialled the number of Bridlington Police Station. She asked to speak to Detective Inspector McMinn, telling the Constable on duty that it was "very important".

"McMinn," came a voice.

"Oh, Inspector McMinn, it's Amanda Raper here, from the Library."

"Hallo there, young lady. What can I do for you?"

"Well, Inspector, I wondered if you knew that the cruise ship in the bay is flying a Panamanian flag?" And she told him all about Robert's news that she had gleaned at lunchtime. "Also, Inspector, I overheard two Germans speaking to a man who looked like Al Capone and they said something about Barclays Bank in the Old Town. Do you think it has anything to do with the body in the Library?"

She felt very excited. She enjoyed reading Detective stories and now she felt that she was taking part in a real one!

"Well, Amanda, I think it only fair to tell you that since this morning there have been one or two developments," said D I McMinn.

He rang off. Amanda went to find her mother who had put the kettle on as requested and had put out two beakers and the tin of chocolate biscuits. It wasn't every day Amanda had something intriguing to tell her!

"Mother, you'll never guess what's happened," exclaimed Amanda and proceeded to relate to her mother the day's events, dramatically emphasising all the gory details. Just as she was finishing her lurid tale the doorbell rang.

"Oh, Inspector McMinn. Please come in. Would you like a cup of tea?"

"I've just been telling my mother all about it, Inspector, I hope you don't mind," she said.

She showed him into the sitting room and asked him to sit down. Mrs Raper brought in a tray with the three beakers full of steaming tea, the biscuit tin and some plates. Amanda introduced her mother to the Detective Inspector and he sat down again, making himself at home.

D I McMinn told his interested audience that when he had seen that the body in the Library had been that of a young man called Harper he had realised that events had overtaken him. He explained Harper was a police informer and had been keeping them in the picture on what he knew about a gang who were planning a bank fraud involving bonds worth trillions of dollars. Bridlington Police had been working in collaboration with Fraud Squad Officers from London and Interpol.

"One document in this fraud had more noughts than I have ever seen on any document in my life!"

Billions of pounds, Deutschmarks, dollars and other currencies were all part of the operation. Harper had found out that some Germans, part of the organisation to set up bogus companies all over the world to launder cash from cocaine and other drugs deals, were aboard a cruise ship. This ship was coming from Norway after visiting the Shetland Isles and going back to the Continent by way of the East Yorkshire Coast. They were to come ashore to meet one of their Italian contacts.

"That was your *man in black*, Amanda," pointed out D I McMinn. "He had been conning wealthy businesses and investment companies to put money into dodgy *paper companies* and all the business had been transacted via the computerised Bridlington office of Barclays Bank in the Old Town.

"Harper must have been sussed. He usually left a telephone message for us at the Police Station and then one of our plain clothes officers would go the Library and see if a note was behind the local books on The Lords Feoffees, (Bridlington's unique charitable organisation) on the shelf in the Reference Library, where those special books are kept. He must have been disturbed this morning by someone who was following him and they stabbed him. The Pathologist says the murder weapon was a knife like those used for gutting fish on board the fishing boats," explained the Inspector. "Now we are looking for someone who works on one of those boats and the knife."

Amanda suddenly remembered the man she had seen furtively stuffing a large package into the postbox that morning. She told the Inspector and he was extremely interested.

"Can you describe him to me, Amanda?"

When she had done so, he asked her to go with him to the Police Station to look at photographs of known criminals and perhaps identify this man.

"We shall need a statement whilst you are there, Amanda, please."

"Thanks for the tea, Mrs Raper. If you don't mind I'll borrow your daughter and we'll see if she can pick out that rogue."

Mrs Raper anxiously said goodbye to Amanda who was too excited to notice her mother's concern. She had never been asked to help the Police with their enquiries before, in fact had never even been inside the Police Station before, so this would be a new experience.

Sergeant Collins went over to the computer and scanned through the records of known men who were possibly connected with the fishing trawlers in Bridlington. He asked Amanda to go through photographs and finally after about an hour she put her finger on one and exclaimed, "That's him, I'm sure!"

"Right, let's have a look then," said Sergeant Collins. "That's Sean Murphy all right. He worked on *The Nancy,* a fishing boat, which went out from the Fish Dock three or four times a week."

He thanked Amanda for her help and saying she should go

home and get her supper, told her, "We'll get him, now!" He left her and went in search of D I McMinn.

Amanda wanted to ring Ian and tell him all about her adventure, then she remembered that he would not be back until late as he had to go to Manchester for the day, in connection with his work. Later that evening, after Amanda and her parents had their evening meal, she watched some television, but could not settle to any of the usual repeats. She took herself off for a long, luxurious soak in the bath and an early night.

The next day Amanda woke early and realised with excitement that it was her birthday and felt that something special should be happening today. She remembered that tonight Ian was taking her to the Flaneburg and perhaps he would *pop the question.* She set off early for work. When she arrived at the Library she found Mr Cooper had made a start clearing up the remainder of the mess. Amanda put the kettle on for the usual first cup of coffee of the day and when Jayne and the other staff arrived they tried to get down to the normal daily business. The telephone rang and it was D I McMinn who said that he was coming in to see them. He had some news!

When he arrived with Sergeant Collins, D I McMinn told his eager audience that early that morning, whilst the fishing boats were waiting for the high tide to set off for the day's fishing, he and Sergeant Collins had gone aboard *The Nancy* and apprehended Sean Murphy. He had tried to get away, but with the help of several Police Officers they had taken him up to the Police Station and questioned him. Ultimately, Sean Murphy had confessed that he had murdered young Harper. He had told them that Harper had overheard him talking to another of the gang and they had decided to *silence* Harper for good. Whilst they were questioning Murphy, Bridlington Post Office had rung to say that a large torn package, had been found by the Postman emptying the postbox outside South Marine Drive Post Office. It was a knife, which they thought looked as though it could be used for gutting fish. Obviously, the Manager thought he should inform the Police.

D I McMinn was very pleased that the mystery of the body in the Library had been solved. "That concludes our case," he told Amanda and her colleagues. "Thank you, Amanda, for your very real help. Because of your awareness we have managed to get our man."

Amanda felt very pleased with herself and could not wait to tell Ian all about it later that evening. And it made the day a very special one, because he did actually ask her to marry him.

In Neutral
by Audrey Bemrose

I stand
Beside the harbour's thick brown mud
And grey silent pools
As shrouding mist blocks the view
Beyond the solid walls.
Sinister seaweed trails from the jetty,
Clinging black-blistered
To the salt-soaked beams.
Rubber-tyred bumpers, heavy as horse collars,
Hang sombrely between rusty patches
On laid up vessels.
Nothing stirs in the out of season gloom.

Two gulls balance delicately on stalk- like legs,
Feet rooted in the harbour bottom,
Feathers neatly laundered
In purest white and softest grey.
They eye me, then cock their heads
As the gentle soothing ripples creep towards them.

The tide turns…. and I walk on.

Message On A Bottle
by Trev Haymer

A wino died today.
The husk of his only comfort remains
Firmly wedged in the prickly maw
Of a white frost-kissed hedge,
Tilted like some polished
Amber tombstone, the thin
Square of pale label
Is his lonely epitaph

Stark skeleton of a green,
Paint-flaked Council bench
In Brid's Old Town was his rigid public bed
A bench squatting hard by a leafless hedge

Where smiling boots greeted
Passers by and spangles of glistening
Drool dripped from the bent wings jaw
Of his Oxfam overcoat
His hair a homeless bird would die for.

Tweed trousers rumpled like some concertina
He still can't see Brid's invisible Marina
Sometimes he'd wave a parchment hand
And flutter black half-moons of yellow nails.
And at night he would stare and tilt
His cold body at the eye of a baleful moon
From the shadow of his cardboard quilt.

'What was that poor man's name?'
A small child asked   her mum.
'Oh him—just a wino—just a bum.'
His life—like the bottle, is non-returnable.

Bridlington
by David Hawkins

Through nine hundred years the Priory Church has gazed down
along the Bayle Gate and High Street
To where, at the quay, the fishing fleet has sailed away at night to
return in early morning
When first light brings the dawning.

Most inhabitants still lie asleep,
Only a few dare take a peep
Through curtains tightly drawn
And ask themselves
"What will you give forth on this brave morn?"

A boy reluctantly awakes
Then demands a bowl of crispy cornflakes:
"Get washed first, wipe that sleep from out your eyes"
And, disinclined, he does arise.

Shopkeepers push up their shutters
As first one and then a flock of seagulls flutters
Through fresh air to spy a fish:
"Now wash up your empty dish
Then get ready for your walk to school
And on the way don't play the fool!"

Cafes open, proprietors arrange their tables and their chairs,
Stand and wait for customers who mostly come in pairs.
Little children holding mothers' hands
Can't wait to reach the sands,
Build castles, then fleeing from sideways moving crabs
Again clutch mothers' hands in fear
But father merely wonders when he'll down his first ice cold
beer.

Still unborn, yet another and another generation
Will rejoice in this magically simple form of recreation.

Bridlington
by Joan Saxby

I do like to write about the seaside
There is such a lot to write about
There's the sea in all its moodiness
Moving from rage to idleness.

The seagulls swooping overhead
Looking for fallen chips and bread
The Yorkshire Belle sails from Bridlington Bay
To Bempton Cliffs every day.

Tourists can see on the cliff tops
Puffins, gannets, and guillemots.
The famous lighthouse at Flamborough Head
Saving sailors from terrible dread.

The walk on the cliff top to Sewerby
With its Hall that stands so proudly
The ice cream vendors throughout the town
The many restaurants that don't let you down.

Old Town with its galleries and history
The Priory Church in its ninth centenary.
The friendliness of people on holiday.
Who all return to Bridlington Bay.

Abridged extracts from 'Sex of the Best'
Two sections of Will Wilcox's story.

He'd been born at Duggleby, a small sparsely populated village high up on the windswept rolling Yorkshire Wolds, and brought up by his Aunt Jill. Their house was only just across the road from the fledgling Gypsey Race, and it was the life-sustaining, crystal-clear waters that bubble free from the underlying chalk a little further up the hill, that had first attracted prehistoric man to the place; indeed Duggleby Howe, the largest prehistoric burial mound in Europe, still remains as proof of their occupation of the area.

From an early age Jill had paid particular attention to Will's oversized appendage, and what with her having never been married, almost inevitably it had developed into a sexual relationship. Eventually they'd followed the course of the Gypsey and moved to Bridlington, but after twenty odd years of love making she'd died, and for the first time in his life Allcock Wilcox was alone.

Ice Cold in Brid
by Will Wilcox

In spite of the weather, or perhaps because of it, I'd forced myself to leave the four walls of my self imposed prison that day. I needed to get out - to blow away the cobwebs. I had to put the past behind me and struggle on without Jill. It was surely time to look to the future; even if I spent the rest of my life sitting around being mawkish, it wouldn't bring her back.

High above the sullen grey clouds, the sun would be shining bright. The narrow strip of golden sand being battered by the surging sea made me think of far off places, far off hot places, where the sand would be too hot to touch ... as it was in the old black and white classic film 'Ice Cold in Alex', that I'd watched on the box the previous night, where an ice-cream, in preference to a lager, would have been gratefully received.... At least by me!

Dream on I thought, in my world it was early March on the East Coast of England.... There were no two ways about it, it was Ice Cold in Brid'.

It would have been oh so easy to have sought solace in the demon drink, but that would have been like taking aspirin for a headache. Not a cure or remedy, but the equivalent of a placebo to dull the senses, and Jill deserved better than to be swept under the magic carpet of an alcoholic binge.

I walked disconsolately along the promenade, leaning into the gale force wind that was once again blowing in off the sea, causing the waves to crash and spume against the harbour wall. Way off on the murky horizon I could see the white-caps churning their displeasure. I dropped onto a bench; today with no other soul in sight I was spoilt for choice. A poem, as yet untitled, that I'd recently finished writing, pestered my tormented brain.

Another day over and wasted away
No laughing and joking or wanting to play
Could I find me a place with a corner to hide?
With my feelings of sadness and hurting inside
Away from the day and away from the night
A secretive place where I'd hide out of sight
Just to think all alone of the six months gone by
Of the hard times and lows of the wherefores and whys
Yet the old clock ticks round to an all brandnew day
Though the sun's shining bright, for me it's just grey
Creeping out of my corner I'm starting to shake
Oh what joy if tomorrow I never should wake?

Fishing for my hanky under the layers of clothing that I'd heaped on to protect me from the biting cold, I wiped the streaming tears from my eyes, together with some errant grains of sand. My thoughts turned to the fishermen beyond the horizon being tossed around at the constant behest of the elements, and I wondered what it was that induced them to take such risks.

Probably I assumed it was the lack of any other work at this time of year. Maybe it was the only way they could make a few quid to provide for their families.... It was almost certainly their last resort. Bridlington in March with the wind in the east.... It had to be the last resort!

The faintest vestige of a strained smile tugged at the corners of my mouth, I begrudgingly noted it as the first evidence of my recovery. Grimly, doggedly I rose from the seat and continued my walk. Every step, like every day of my life now that Jill had gone, was a battle. Sometimes bracing myself against a strong gust, other times lurching forward, as a lull in the wind caught me out. I felt and must have looked like a matchstick man straining against the elements in one of L. S. Lowry's paintings.

I directed my faltering footsteps towards the comparative shelter of the harbour and viewed the motley collection of small brightly coloured boats that languished high and dry on the oozing mud, that was fast being covered by the incoming tide. At the far end of the harbour, under the modern boat hoist, the Gypsey betrayed its presence, as its waters swirled and mingled with the muddy salt water, in the channel its flow had created over many centuries. At last free from the last mile of its tortuous twisting journey through the Town, and free from its gravel bed, blighted by the Neanderthal members of the community who welcomed its crystal-clear waters by using it as a repository for all manner of rubbish. Evidently they appeared to get some weird kick from mistreating the stream in this way. I wondered what it was that made them different from normal folk. If irrefutable evidence of their lack of brain cells were needed, it was unnecessary to look any further than the number of shopping trolleys that they seemed to never tire of throwing in.

Turning away with my unspoken sad thoughts, I headed inland towards the modern shopping arcade.... Maybe a hot cup of tea might raise my flagging spirits. Still the mischievous wind buffeted me around as I slowly progressed up Chapel Street. Small whirlpools of debris swirled and circled my feet, some no doubt dropped by accident or snatched from cold fingers by the unrelenting wind, but mostly simply discarded by the same brain-dead cretins who thought it was their god-given right to sully the Gypsey.

It was an ongoing mystery to me, why the right thinking majority of the community allowed it to continue unchecked. To my mind, instead of the Council paying to have the rubbish cleaned up, they should see it as a source of income, and employ half a dozen muscular out of work bodybuilders to issue on the spot swingeing fines. I was sure that our streets would soon be as pristine clean as those of Austria and Switzerland.

Almost blown off my feet I staggered through the automatic sliding doors. At last, a respite from the cold wind. To catch my breath, I entered one of the shops. Just to give me time to compose myself before going for the cup of tea.... Just to kill a little time ... while time was killing me. My thoughts of hot drinks however, were soon banished from my mind as the overwhelming blast of hot air from the heaters above my head had me unzipping my cagoule and tugging at my muffler. Forget the tea; an ice-cream was what I needed now more than anything else.

I sidled up to the brightly painted handcart, with its impressive array of flavours already on display, no doubt in early anticipation of the hoards of Easter holidaymakers to come. After a moment's thought I plumped for a strawberry cornet ... and no I didn't want a flake stuck in it thank you very much. The Beatles' *Strawberry Fields For Ever* rattled around in my head; next month the car boot sales would start up again on Brid's Strawberry Fields. I paid the young woman and, admiring her shapely legs, licked my ice-cream ... maybe the future wouldn't be so bad after all; maybe at last I really was on the mend! ... Maybe next time I'd give her Tutti-frutti a try.

We Are Family!
by Will Wilcox

Time had slipped by almost unnoticed; I'd been going to the local writers' group for almost a year and it was already April 2013. Possibly unlucky for some, and undoubtedly that would be the case for those who lived on the seabed, beyond the newly extended sewage outfall. Out of sight out of mind best described their plight. Inland however, after another long winter, the new shoots of spring were valiantly struggling to show themselves. Everywhere had an air of pent-up anticipation about it, as the plant life waited to burst forth and entertain the section of society I thought of as the watchers. I on the other hand was a doer, and the task that we'd been set was to write a short story centred on Brid.

Bridlington, it was indeed a broad canvas that we'd been given to paint our pictures on. However the days were relentlessly ticking closer to the next monthly meeting and still nothing had provoked me to put pen to paper. I wondered if maybe I was losing my literary touch…. As well!

I'd always thought of writing as an art form in its own right. My pen the brush, my notepad the canvas, and the paint and stories…. Well! – Mostly nothing more than 'pigments' of my imagination…. Eventually, as the mountain wouldn't come to my desk, I decided to go to the mountain, by way of the coach park that occupies a large area of the former Railway Carriage Sidings on Hilderthorpe Road.

On weekends long gone, and especially on Bank Holidays, it would have been jam packed with railway carriages that had brought the holidaymakers in their droves. They would gather from all corners of Yorkshire's three Ridings and beyond, to indulge themselves in all that Brid' could offer. But time had moved on and, with a little help from Dr Beeching, the road transport lobby and their political lackeys, not to mention the advent of cheap foreign holidays, the flow of visitors to the town had diminished considerably, although not to such a great extent as experienced by many other seaside towns.

It was a fact that many of the visitors that came to the town were repeat offenders who came year after year, but nowadays invariably arrived by coach or private car. I laconically thought of the virtual demise of the railways as perhaps just another dubious example of 'progress in motion' that did no one any credit.

Leaning against a concrete post by the pedestrian access in the boundary fence, I sucked on a mint and patiently waited for the first coach to arrive. As is often the case where buses are concerned, two arrived together; their front tyres circumscribing a large semicircle on the concrete surface, before they both came shuddering to a halt side by side. As the air-brakes were applied, in unison they emitted a noise suggesting that any further would have been a day trip too far. The swirling brightly coloured script adorning the rear end of the nearest bus informed me that its home town was Doncaster.

Showing no prejudice, I carefully evaluated its motley selection of day trippers as they disgorged, stretching, yawning and farting into the welcoming morning air…. They silently shouted, 'Look out Brid' we're here, ready or not. I was certain that among this diverse collection of humankind, there would be a story as yet unarticulated waiting to be told.

A woman, I calculated to be in her mid-twenties, caught my eye. Slim, fresh complexion showing no signs of makeup, shoulder length fair hair with a natural wave, and apparently alone. She was wearing a canary yellow bolero style jacket unbuttoned, with a dazzlingly white blouse open at the neck, and a tight pale blue-green skirt cut just above the knee. As she came down the steps, the hem had ridden up showing a goodly amount of thigh. Ladylike, but in no hurry, she smoothed the offending garment back into place with a small hand consisting of short fingers with neatly trimmed fingernails, all unadorned by nail polish.

On stepping onto terra-firma, she squinted at the brightness of the day as though looking for a welcoming committee. No doubt disappointed, she rummaged in her shoulder bag and, in a moment, produced a fancy pair of pink sunglasses, which she perched with a flourish on the tip of her turned up little nose. Personally I thought that they clashed with the canary yellow of her jacket, but what did I know when it came to such things? My expertise lay elsewhere. One step away from the bus and she was gathering her tiny coat around her as though the temperature was dropping off the scale. Giving what might be construed as an affected shiver, she headed in my direction giving off all the vibes of an ultra efficient office secretary. I couldn't help but notice that she went in and out in all the right places and was of 'pleasing' proportions. Her white high heeled shoes added an extra something to her general demeanour, making as pleasant a picture as anyone with an eye for the ladies could wish for; however as nice as she was to gaze upon, somehow I didn't think she would figure in my story.

As though on castors she came abreast of me, and I quipped that if the local ambient temperature wasn't to her liking, maybe if she went down south, that might bring a little colour to her cheeks. Her lips parted and curled as if searching for a suitably cutting response, but behind the shades her features showed no sign of emotion one way or the other, however she shortened her stride pattern and turning her head asked, 'Was that supposed to be a euphemism for getting between your legs?' I suggested, with a roguish twinkle, that it was as much of a euphemism as she wanted it to be.

As she continued her perambulation towards the toilet block, over her shoulder a short salvo of friendly fire spurted from her lips and whistled past my right ear ... 'M-a-y-b-e l-a-t-e-r.' Unmoved, my attention remained on the passengers and, as prophesied, my eyes alighted on one trio who stood out from the crowd. This was more like it! Father ... short of stature but built like a brick outhouse, showing no signs of a neck, but more than making up for it with his bulging beer-belly. Florid complexion, hair thinning on top, T-shirt, clearly retaining the memory of breakfast down the front; brawny arms festooned with tattoos proclaiming his undying love for Mary, Susan and Tanya. Stubby grimy toes protruding from brown latticework sandals, his broken nails adorned with crudely painted George flags.... Every picture, as they say, tells a story!

Mother, thin as a rake, unkempt hair, sallow complexion, shrunken woolly jumper draped around pinched shoulders, large holdall in one hand ... overflowing with everything but the kitchen sink, and who could say that somewhere under all the Pac-a-macs, towels, Spam sandwiches and extra large bottles of Coke there wasn't even one of those.

Her other hand was being fully occupied trying to keep tousle-haired little Johnny in check. I surmised that, without fail, even the passengers that were hard of hearing would be sick to the back teeth of having had to listen to, 'Stop that Johnny,' 'No Johnny,' 'If you do that one more time Johnny I'll ...,' and so on and so on. You've met 'em! Straining at the leash, spotty articles full of preservatives and never happy unless they're unhappy, dressed in a vertically striped T-shirt making him look for all the world like a stick of rock with Dennis the Menace impressed all the way through. I could see that it was just a matter of time! Little Johnny was an accident waiting to happen. And so, pushing the Canary's tenuous promise of 'Maybe Later' to the back of my mind, I decided, ready or not, Johnny would be my April story.

Falling in line behind them I stood at the traffic lights waiting for the green man to beckon us over. Mother, fed up with her offspring's pulling and tugging, let go of his hand and gave him a hefty swipe around the ear. Johnny, propelled by the velocity of the clout lurched out into the road. With a long telescopic arm fully extended, I just managed to drag him back onto the pavement as White Van Man sped by, oblivious to the near miss. Father stood equally oblivious in a world of his own, absentmindedly exploring his right nostril with his little finger.

I felt a certain empathy for the boy that was destined not to last. I couldn't help but wonder how he'd survived this long. Mother only tut-tut-ed and gave Johnny another one for good measure, before grabbing his hand once more. She was clearly a female multi-tasker that I'd heard so much of; they were apparently able to talk the hind leg off a donkey while doing the ironing, cooking the dinner, planning the next family holiday, and giving anyone in earshot a bollocking for something they hadn't done, all simultaneously without breaking sweat. I guessed that it must be an evolutionary thing handed down by their mothers, and their mothers before them.

Almost soundlessly the Yellow Canary appeared at my side, and nudging me in the ribs with her elbow said, 'Is everything as big as your mouth then, or is that the extent of your talents?' She clearly had had time to think of a suitable rejoinder, and she certainly knew how to hit a man when he was trying to concentrate on other things. I said that I'd never been a person who needed to brag about such things, but that if she would like to stick around until I'd finished my present business, she might find out at first hand....

The lights changed and, sheep-like, we all trooped across to the narrow broken pavement beyond, that led down the road to the seafront. It was a rundown area of the town earmarked for modernisation, yet doggedly it still clung to the past, however one sensed that its grip was loosening. It would almost certainly only be a matter of time before the bulldozers moved in and did their worst – or best if you prefer your towns to be architecturally identical, as seems the modern way of doing things.

The very first shop containing cheap plastic whatnots that Johnny spotted had him on tiptoes with nose pressed up against the window, stamping and yelling, 'I want! I want!' Then he noticed the bright green inflatable dingy dangling on a string by the shop door and his heart was set; if he didn't get one of those everybody's day would descend into one long day trip of misery. Already, at such a young age, Johnny was a past master at playing one parent against the other and as usual it was only a matter of minutes before he got his own way.

The threesome, only pausing to pick up ice creams and candyfloss, rushed headlong down the steps to the strip of beach, where the travel rug was soon spread and they set up camp. I leant against the promenade railings above, just behind their pitch, and viewed the scene. There was a broad strip of wet sand in evidence, clearly the tide was going out, and it had turned into a comfortably warm day for a change. I was aware that the Canary was loitering with intent a little way off; dedicated to getting the best story, I decided that she could always be a second string to my bow if Johnny didn't come up trumps. Like a reporter on the trail of a good story, I hurriedly scribbled a few observations in my notebook and stuffed it back in my pocket.

As Johnny pulled on his bathing trunks, I pondered whether or not to give the family the benefit of my local knowledge. The wind was blowing off the land, as was invariably the case when the temperature was above freezing on the East Coast. Should I point out the inherent dangers of going to sea in a pea-green boat? And that such a flimsy thing would quickly be swept out beyond the harbour wall, where strong currents would make off with it and little Johnny both. I struggled with my conscience, trying to couch a sentence in my head that might convey the urgency of the situation. I could hear the words clearly enough, 'Sorry to be a party-pooper, but don't you think it might be prudent to stop Johnny…? Maybe better safe than sorry would be the best axiom to apply in this case …?' But the words somehow never left my lips; you see the truth of the matter was that I needed Johnny to be swept out to sea for my story, and in all honesty it was no more than the shifty snivelling snotty-nosed little sod deserved….

By the time I'd made up my mind, the pea-green boat was already well beyond the paddlers and swimmers and was heading for deep water at a rate of knots. I was telling myself it wasn't my fault and even if I had voiced my fears, they would unquestionably have fallen on deaf ears, or in Father's case, deaf cauliflower ears. In spite of all this, the feeling that I'd shirked my responsibilities prevailed and, breaking into a run, I set off for the harbour wall. Glancing back I caught a glimpse of Canary, nonplussed and flapping her wing ... arms in frustration. Pushing through the crowd I grabbed a lifebelt and raced along its length to the harbour entrance ... just in time to see Johnny go floating by.

There was only one thing I could do - if the current was taking the boat that way ... well ... I took a deep breath and, clinging to the lifebelt, jumped in. Luckily the sea was fairly calm, so using my right arm as a paddle I set off in hot pursuit only to find that it was a misnomer, a contradiction in terms. The water was as cold as the hearts of the pipeline planners. In no time at all we were off Flamborough Head. I'd just about caught up with Johnny, so I shouted, 'Chin up lad, good view of the cliffs from here; best make the most of it eh? Just think, it'll probably be a once in a lifetime experience!' Then I heard the helicopter from Leconfield overhead, it must have been on standby at Filey Brigg; it seemed that Johnnie perpetually lived a charmed life. As they winched him to safety, the under-tow carried me off....

I was just clearing Stottle Bank Nook when the strangest thing happened. I could hear a tiny persistent piping voice that seemed to emanate from far below, or it may have been the cold salt water affecting my brain.... But whatever the case it went something like this ...

We are Family ...

We're only poor little crustaceans
Who live way down under the sea
We've never been 'prawn' to complaining
But hope you take heed of our plea

Oh dear. It's not in our nature
We're all part of life's tapestry
But somebody just had to speak out
Life once was worth living you see

We never start wars or cause trouble
We're just a small cog in the chain
We've managed for millions of years
But lately we're feeling the strain

We accept that you're going to catch us
And eat us in salads and such
But the latest humiliation
Is simply a little too much

I think our days may be numbered
For humans are causing us pain
We're up to our necks in big trouble
Thanks to all that goes down the drain

I'm exceedingly under the weather
Came down with a terrible cough
The sun might be shining where you are
But I'm feeling really browned off

We don't like to think of extinction
Dinosours didn't think it much fun
A better approach might just save us
But be quick for the 'job's' almost done

So next time you flush, spare a moment
To think of young molluscs at sea
For things have turned rather nasty
Please don't do the dirty on me.

My strength, like the tide, was fast ebbing away; I thought I'd had my chips and was about to let go of the lifebelt when I was pulled from the water by the chopper…. I guess it could have been worse …. But not much!

Bridlington Priory
by Lesley Ince

Carved Angels

Which great oaks were felled for you?
What hand feathered your wings,
carved the soft folds of your drapery?
Let harps sound, bells ring
and trumpets blaze, lifted by angels
that sing out truth as they stand guard
over human voices raised to God.

Lectern

Men stand on a platform behind you
reaching the congregation
with words from the open bible.
The eagle, God's creature,
is wrought in brass,
carries His words on spread wings
channelling peace and hope.

Pews

We are here to give you support
for your troubles. Lower yourselves
to rest on us. Sit your pain,
bring your joy. We are God's furniture
in God's house.
Be still.
Hold faith in your open lap.

Celebrations
by Joan Saxby

Let's celebrate because we're here
With Yorkshire fare and Yorkshire beer
Let's celebrate, go out to dine
With Brid. seafood and dry white wine.

Let's celebrate a special day
In Bridlington's historic bay
They're going to do this nice town up
With taste we hope; to that we'll sup.

To the future of our town
Dear planners do not let us down
And when the building dust has settled
Let's celebrate again that we've been fettled.

Beyond our town, a magic year
Hip hip hurray I want to hear
For Queen Liz 2 in her diamond year
For Brit Olympians give a cheer.

Let's be thankful we live here
In this town and country I hold dear
Raise your glass of wine or beer
And for our people give a cheer.

Our weather may be oft erratic
One thing's for sure, it is not static
But we can all so proudly stand
In this our green and pleasant land.

Seaside Treats at Bridlington
by Michael Perry

In Princes Street, Bridlington the brightest shop was the 'Best Italian Ice Cream Emporium in England'. Its highly-illuminated, inside seating area a mass of gold fittings and plush red leather chairs and stools. The staff, all with funny accents and big smiles, would coax you in off the footpath to try 'our dill-lish-housea, hice greamaa'.

The pictures of the different types and prices displayed on boards were extra eye-catching persuaders. The counter display cabinets were full of a multitude of rainbow-coloured and flavoured treats. All the various toppings in tubs, jars and bottles, shining in the glow of well-placed spotlights, were more attention grabbers. They stopped your legs moving but made your eyes and mouth pop wide open.

It was here at the age of four and a half, and cousin Shirley now three and a half, we attempted our very first Knickerbocker Glory. Dressed in Sunday best and being well behaved we deserved a special treat that day, out with parents and all the family. The tall glass vases were so high we had to stand on the seats to reach the top. In our hands giant-handled spoons as long as your arms. Cream, chocolate, nuts, ice cream, fruit, some of which we had never tried before like Pineapple, Peach, Mango, added to the colourful sweet mass we keenly spooned into our smiling mouths and around our faces.

I can't remember if we ate it all or were helped, but after the special feast a walk was in order. Near the ice cream parlour stood the impressive fishing harbour. It was here we saw and smelt the adults' delight of mussels, cockles, whelks and prawns all awaiting the seasoning of salt, pepper and vinegar to enhance the taste. I remember trying the gritty, salty, rubber band fruit of the sea proffered by each adult. All different sizes and colours, yet they all seemed to taste the same.

On the harbour wall walkway the costumed Gypsy

fortune-tellers, clanking penny machines, the stall barkers shouting out, "win a goldfish or teddy bear", or "just knock a coconut off the stand", or "dart a card sir", while the loud music made it hard to hear anything clearly.

The train ride in brightly painted livery on its circuit of rails through the scenes of Alice in Wonderland attracted and carried us, to our delight and the photograph-taking pleasures of the adults. Beyond this more stalls of foods and drinks. The smell of fresh hot donuts, the ladies' delight. Well the men had had their seafood, so the donuts were for the women and of course we children didn't miss out on those either.

Next the flying chairs high in the air, going faster and faster and higher and higher. The world appeared spinning beneath our dangling legs. There's the sea, the harbour, the train ride, uncles, town, people, sand, sea, harbour, train uncle town sand sea harbour people town sand sea harbour train sea harbour town sand sea sky, sick. Oh, I want to get off.

We've had a lovely day; can we do it again tomorrow?

Echoes Of Summer
by Trev Haymer

This sea is restless now, brown and batherless
In the harsh grey month of November.

She longs for the ice-cream bosoms,
The flaky limbs and flaying hands
Of nerve-frayed parents whose red bawling
Offspring challenge the screaming gulls.

She longs for the smoky chippie stalls,
The 'kiss me quick' hats, the whoops
From the yellow throat of the gaunt
Helter-skelter whose gaping maw twisted
Young screams in a hot sun and now
Bites on a grid of iron.

She listens for the whispers of hand-clasping
Lovers bonded like curved mussels—
Black shadows under the glistening pier.

This sulking sea now beckons the grateful stride
Of a lone runner whose swift eyes bear the stain
Of a salt-edged wind. He kicks the bleached sole
Of a long lost sandal, flicking it into her slack maw.

She gulps it greedily, grinds it in her pebbly throat
And listens—hears these echoes of summer.

A Bridlington Bird
by Ken Joul

The window opens and frightens me off the ledge. No wonder we are becoming angry birds. We herring gulls were here on this land before you humans came and built your cave dwellings, creating turbulent winds between them. And why do you have to call us seagulls; that is not our proper name. We have tried to live alongside your dwellings in harmony, but now you consider us to be vermin. I mean, that is the lowest of the low and we are creatures of a higher domain. Now you cover your roofs with nets and put spiky things on ledges to deter us from landing or even building our nests. We need to breed just as you humans do.

Many a time all we want to do is stand and rest on your properties and survey around to see what is going on or who might be putting food out for us. Yes there are humans who do like to look after us and we thank you.

Well I am tired of flying around this windy day and so I will have to find somewhere to feed. Once again it will have to be on the water as there are no humans eating things along the closed in water's edge offering titbits. I'll just land here on top of this thing that lifts your floating contraptions out of the water; at least they have not put spikes there. Ah, that feels good; a flick of the wings and tail feathers and I am comfortable. Now where is there going to be some food?

Ah-ha, the tide is in and I have never seen so much water coming down what you call the Gypsey Race for a long time. Surge out, meeting surge in, creates disturbance on the seabed. Yes, there we are, the ducks are having a field day so I will go and join them. Here we go; that made them quack. Oh yes, a few tasty bits for the taking; one gulp each and it's gone but so have the ducks, which are no longer disturbing the bottom. Ah well; off to find somewhere else.

Tide coming in must mean some tasty morsels being made available. I'll go and join my kinsmen and swim on the water. There's a small crab; not fast enough mate. That makes a tasty starter. A small fish; a dart of the beak and it's mine. A little larger than I thought; took two gulps to get it down. What's that wriggling away under the surface? Ugh, that caught me out. It was just some rubbish that you humans had thrown away. I think I was a little late for the feast, so time to move on again.

A beautiful take-off, if I say it myself, but where to go. I'll just ride the wind and see what takes my fancy. Ah-ha, my friends on the sea have not noticed it. Maybe I'll be the first there. One of your floating human things that is specially made for catching fish. That is supposed to be our staple diet but you humans also seem intent on taking that away from us. Another reason for us to be angry and intent on finding other sources of food from the rubbish you leave around. Sometimes those things prepare the fish or throw little ones back. Let's have a see what they are doing. That's lucky, I can see that they have left some things behind; here goes for a guzzle.

Now I feel over full; well none of my friends came to help, not that I called them. That is another thing you humans complain about; the noise we make. But we only cry to the sky to warn other birds off our patch. We don't really like to be crowded together, but you people make it so we have to by making some of our nesting sites no-go areas. Mind you my mate found a good nesting site. Used it last year for the first time and we will use it again. Woe betides any other bird that tries to take it; they will feel the strength of my beak. It is on a little ledge that is hidden from human eyes by a metal thing that sometimes gives off strange smells.

Well that's enough reminiscing whilst that food has been digesting. Floating around here is no good as it will not be long before the sun goes down. Better get back to shore as the tide will be leaving shortly and should leave more goodies for feasting. Up, up and away, but what's that I see? A group of humans walking along the closed in water area and eating things from their hands. Better check it out. Ah, I see some of the younger gulls already have and those pesky pigeons are trying to get in on the act.

Well I am definitely the better looking of those birds and not the dowdy brown of the juveniles. If I land on the wall and look my best, maybe they will throw something my way. Wow, I did not even have to land before something was thrown in the air and I caught it with a little aerobatics. Here we go again. Damnation, I missed that, but it seems to have amused them and here we go again. Not so fast, I can only chase one thing at a time. Now I come to think, it tastes like the smell from the metal at my nesting site. Still, it's food and easily found, but not as good as the raw fish you humans have in those funny dishes. They really do tempt some of us to fly right up to you and take directly from the dish. Even better when you take fright and drop all the contents for us to enjoy as you run away.

Time to land and see if they will feed me more. Oops, time to move off. One of those hairy brutes you humans have is getting too close for comfort. Back to the edge of the sea for the dark period. I can see movement in the water in the dark and will be able to snack until the light is back with us.

The light is now back and it was a pleasant interlude chatting with my mate with whom I had a good chick rearing score last year and hopefully we will again this year as we swam and ate together. Sometimes there is safety in numbers, although we tend to keep our distance from one another as we are not that sociable a bird. But now the wind is steady; time to ride it, so farewell my friends until the next time. Today, like all other days, it is every bird for himself where food is concerned. Fantastic, stretch the wings and just soar and then gently glide before a beat of the wings takes you higher. Nothing like it. The higher you go and circle lazily, the more you can see.

Got to keep body and soul together and for that more food is required. Need to keep a weather eye open for something.

What's that moving over there on land? Must be interesting as some of my brethren are already circling. Time to join them. Oh good, one of you humans has a thing that is clawing up the ground. Bound to be plenty of good pickings. Here we go and quick as a flash I am down among the turned over ground. Wriggly things, grubs, old roots, wonderful, a feast fit for any bird.

Too many birds now and we are all fighting over anything on the surface. It is time I moved on. I need to gain height again to see what else is available. Flap, flap and we are away; letting the wind take me where it will. I remember this place. More of your built caves, but with open ground outside. I'm sure, ah yes there it is, one of your human plots where I found some white stuff that had been thrown out. There is something, but it is not white, although those little birds are having a field day. Soon spoil that, here we go and land right in the middle of them, although some scattered as soon as my shadow appeared.

Not bad stuff, but it was brown with hard bits in it. It sticks a little in the craw. Need some water to wash it down and then I will be back. Up in the air again and there in another plot is water. Down we go and land. Oops, that edge was slippy and I have ended up in the water itself. Maybe that other lot over there will be better as I have stirred this up. A quick look around, but no-one approaching so beak in and swallow. A few more like that and I am ready to eat again.

Obviously the humans here do not like me as the goodies for birds have been put in cages and placed where I cannot reach. I cannot hover and webbed feet make it impossible to clutch onto anything small. Mind you, I did get one up on a similar place as they had put some fatty morsel out for the floor eating birds and I found it and took it in one gulp. Hee, hee. Let's see if there is anything of that brown stuff left. Oh no; the other birds have taken it all. Ah well, I will just land on this cave top and strut my stuff up and down. A quick shout to the sky will let everyone know it is my place for now, including that youngster. It is no good peeping and bowing to me as I am not about to regurgitate anything for you.

There was wet out of the sky last night and a nice green area down there. I wonder if the wriggly things will come out for me. Here we go; a launch and glide down with a quick flip of wings and tail to alight gently. Nothing obvious around so I will have to persuade them to come to the top. All I need to do is stamp my feet and up they come. Don't know why they do it, but it never fails. There's one, gulp and another with more over there; this really is a feast.

That is all I need. Those horrible terns have increased their numbers no end; where they breed is further up the coast, but now they seem to be trying to horn in on our territories. Life is so unfair as you humans think they are a prettier bird than us; being smaller with not as big a beak. They really are common.

As a big bird with a nasty beak, we have few predators, except when we have eggs or chicks. You humans, however, keep a stealthy one. We always have to keep an eye open for them trying to creep up on us when we are on the ground. There is one big black one over there looking my way; I'll turn so I can watch. Yes, I thought so; here it comes trying to keep hidden behind anything larger than itself. Now let's see who is the better. A quick rush on its part, but I am ready and go to meet it at the last minute. A quick peck to the head and I am away and airborne. One to me. And yes, we will attack you if we feel our nests or chicks are in danger from you, but this is only rare. We can mostly tell if you are posing a danger to us.

Now where can I find more food? Over there, young humans are leaving one large cave and going into one, two, no three others. That can only mean one thing, they are grubbing for food too and usually very wasteful they are. That's it, here they come eating out of something and there we have the first throw away. Down we go to find out what. Don't know but it tastes alright. Oh dear, others of my kin have seen me dive and have come to join me and I can see others on the way. It's going to be a free-for-all shortly. Mind you, they are welcome to it. Mostly it is white stuff encased in a shell, which won't break when we try to drop it like shellfish. These crack open when dropped onto a rock and leave the lovely flesh exposed.

I'll have that; no brown, streaky juvenile is going to take the food out of my mouth. There they go following the crowd, but I have learnt a few things and know that it is not unusual for there to be latecomer humans and here we have two. I'll follow them but keep low. If you don't want that, I'll have it thank you. I'm not sure about the things your food came out of, but I once saw one of those damned big black birds shake something out of one so I will try my luck. Ah yes, there it is. To you humans it might seem insignificant, but I'll not turn my beak up at it. Another, but nothing in it; ah well you win some you lose some.

The Memory of an Elephant
by Julia Oldham

Our family had a holiday in Bridlington for three consecutive years during the eighties. The first two years were full of sea, sand, donkey rides, hot weather, motorboat rides in the pool by the Spa theatre, and a trip out to sea on a pleasure boat to view the white cliffs.

Unfortunately, the third year was spent in the rain - fishing in the rock pools, swimming in Leisure World, and only one day spent on the beach, which turned out fairly warm. After all, this is what holidays are all about - sandcastles and fizzy pop when you are nearly starting infant school. Both sons were fratchy all week. We put it down to the weather, but they woke up covered in spots on the day of departure. The chickenpox plague had finally caught up with them.

One not-so-rainy day, the whole family walked to the green parkland near Sewerby, where a circus had pitched for the week. We arrived early and peered at the llamas, a solitary tiger with doleful eyes, and grey horses, through the bright red bars of the old trailers. We sat in the big top on plastic seats, breathing in the musty smell of damp grass, enjoying the clowns, the trapeze artists and somersaulting, sequined, acrobatic ladies on the galloping grey horses. The final act, prior to the interval, were the performing elephants and we were finally relieved of our misery. The last elephant leaving the ring also relieved itself. How our youngest son roared with laughter as the animal-keeper shovelled up the excrement - one lump per spadeful!!

This year, we took our grandchildren to a human circus. Their laughter was not as forthcoming as that four year old boy, nearly thirty years ago.

The Ice Cream Vendor
by Joan Saxby

Oh to be an ice cream vendor
Selling ice creams all day long
Keeping cool behind that window
Playing out the ice cream song.

Not just one Cornetto
Here I have it all
I know you won't regretto
Come visit at my stall.

Vanilla, chocolate, raspberry ripple,
Strawberry, lemon or Neopolitan
What ice cream flavour is your tipple?
What joy to see the ice cream van!

If you are fond of pistachio
You'll find it's green and nutty
The bits get into one's mustachio
But it's better than a sweet jam butty.

If today you're pleasure seeking
Try my creamy caramel
Let me set your taste buds ticking
I've every taste to ring your bell.

Don't go home until you've tried it
Try a few, I've tastes galore
You'll come back, I'll guarantee it
Asking for to try some more.

Sunny days are all I ask for
So I'll get rich and make my pile
In Winter when you're all behind your door
I'll be sailing up the Nile!

The Feminine Touch
by Audrey Bemrose

Bridlington is a matronly sort of town. A motherly, familiar, friendly woman; reliable, always there when you want her. Her open arms will clasp you to her bosom, whilst you pour out your troubles.

She settles down comfortably by the beach, froths of foam edging her underskirt as the oncoming tide gently laps round her feet, easing the aches and soothing her painful corns.

Like her mother before her she welcomes whole generations of families and friends to sit beside her as they turn their backs on industrial grime, and she encourages them to look out over the waves, breathing in the revitalizing air of the bay.

Her grandmothers too spent their days nourishing the needs of others. One, the 'Old Town' landlady, provided beer and wholesome meals for carriers and farmers coming to the weekly markets. The other, down at 'Quay', baited fishing lines, and sold ice cream and jugs of tea while Edwardian ladies strolled on The Parade listening to the orchestra, and children in sailor suits watched pierrots and Punch and Judy on the beach. Families are her life.

She still has the white shoulders of a young girl, glimpsed as the sunlight catches the chalk of Flamborough Head, but she feels the cold a little more now, and wraps the edge of the soft green shawl of the Wolds around her. Others may prefer to dip their toes in distant oceans, but she likes to stay with what is familiar.

The fashions in her wardrobe range from Victorian terrace houses and small hotels to jarring eyesores of the seventies. Attempts to keep up with the times do not sit well on her ample figure, and here and there her best outfits are stained and torn - evidence of one or two mad flings and accidents whilst in unsuitable company. But now the lengthening days give her the impetus to look her best. She tries on her new spring suit, cocks her head jauntily and smiles as she looks in the mirror of progress and prepares for the next generation to come home.

Time's Shadow
by Trev Haymer

Listen – and you will hear the morning
Splash of these sleep-sodden feet
Shuffling a tar-black road.

See – the slumbering tramp wrapped in
Yesterday's news – kids walking to school,
A crocodile in the maw of a zebra.

Hear – the coarse yawn of the yellow-breasted
crossing patroller – the rasp of a thin dog sliding by –
Like me, his shadow tilts.

Feel – the blink of time's eyeball
Counting the blur of shrivelling years,
Every hour spills fast grains.

Watch – a sliver of sun pierce the skin
Of this porridge sky – the dance of gold
Leaves on the knarled feet of a tall tree.

Tonight – I will walk in Brid bay's wind,
I'll curve like a young tree, I'll drift along
The curled edge of the sharp wind's tongue
Whose salty breath will lick the skin of my nostrils.
I'll crouch beneath the gaze of a young moon
Whose half-smile floods wrinkled sand
Wet with the spittle of a sulking sea,
And I'll feel old as the distant hills
Crowding my tired shoulder.

I'll listen to the restless silence
Of this sleeping town, hear only baby-cries
Of late gulls, then, painted by the moon's silver eye
I may see time's bent shadow.

Hats Off To Holidays
by Patricia Susan Dixon MacArthur

I saw her coming down the road as soon as she turned the corner. She looked like the kind of toadstool Alice might have encountered in Wonderland.

"Well? What do you think Jo?" she asked me, a beaming smile plastered across her face as she twirled like a schoolgirl.

Why had she bought a flipping sombrero? It was huge. I would go so far as to say it was enormous. "It's a little bigger than I expected," I said.

"Is that all you have to say? What about the colours?" she glowed with pride.

Awful, I thought. "Unusual," I said.

"I think you mean it's unique. Just like me!"

"I don't really think unique does it justice," I said. "If Pablo Picasso had ever created a large sun hat this would most definitely be it. There are so many colours."

"Such beautiful, cheerful colours don't you think?"

No. No. No. Whatever were you thinking? I wondered, but I said, "Well there's a band of every shade of colour you could imagine starting at the brim with shocking pink, then lime green, yellow, electric blue, scarlet, white ..."

"I know it's perfect isn't it? Colour is just what we need after all we've been through. I am going to live what's left of my life to the full and enjoy every moment."

I didn't want to remember how sick she'd been. All her hair fell out when she had chemotherapy. We couldn't have done this last year.

"It's very big," I squeaked. She was right though, we did both need some colour in our lives. Her illness had brought total greyness with edging shades of black.

"The brim will keep the sun off my face, I burn so easily as you know."

"It's quite a tall hat isn't it?" I said.

"It's a perfect fit and so snug to wear."

Did the person who sold it to you hypnotise you first? I wanted to ask. "That's good then," I croaked, my voice giving way. If it made her happy I was happy for her, it was time our luck changed. I wasn't going to think about the unopened letters we had both left behind at home. Had I got a place at uni? If I'd got a place would I want to go away and leave her? What was her letter from the hospital about? Let's enjoy our day out together and then read our letters when we get home, she'd said. Today we shall be carefree tourists without a worry in the world. I'd agreed completely, glad to have this time just for us, although, I hadn't expected her to buy the hat on the way to meet me. She didn't usually want to be noticed, or stand out from the crowd, but her vibrant pink skirt and purple t-shirt made her conspicuous today. Like me she was fairly quiet natured most of the time, we usually liked the same things. People were staring at her now, at least I thought they were, she'd probably not have agreed with me. This sudden need of hers to hide from the sun was new. To be fair she did turn lobster-red quite easily so it was understandable. But she'd never have dressed like this before.

"Let's have a walk on the seafront," I suggested. The sooner I get you off the street the better I thought. She'd be less noticeable down there. I felt mean for thinking it. I was just glad she was still alive. Did a daft hat really matter?

"Good idea," she agreed readily.

We couldn't afford to go away for a holiday this year, so we'd decided to be tourists in Bridington our home town. We'd already been to all the local attractions; you forget how much there is to do on your own doorstep. These were all the places I'd loved as a small child and it was wonderful to take the time to revisit them together. No airport lounges or traffic jams for us thank you very much.

It was such a beautiful day and I loved to be on Bridlington seafront. No sooner had we made our way on to the promenade than we smelled the frying onions of the burger bar, followed by the sweet vanilla of the donuts, but it was the stomach-tugging aroma of fish and chips we gave in to. Our lunch was lovely. We sat on a bench and looked at the vast stretch of sparkling blue sea, watching boats of different types and sizes, some far away on the horizon, others nearer to shore, like the speedboat that raced across the water. We heard the laughter and excited shrieks of children playing on the beach below us. Donkeys gave rides to small, eager children who tentatively approached their chosen animal with palms outstretched in introduction. Seagulls swooped upon every morsel of discarded food, but today even they looked pure and white in the sunshine. To my relief we blended in down here; a lot of people wore brightly coloured holiday clothing and sun hats, small normal-sized ones.

"What a beautiful world we live in," she said. "It's great to be alive."

I totally agreed. Fortunately we'd just about finished eating when the sky went black and the first big drops of rain fell. The cloud had crept up behind us and spread over our heads, it would soon cover the sun. People began to move, some putting umbrellas up, others gathering discarded children's clothes into bags whilst the youngsters continued paddling.

"Let's head across the harbour path to the café for a coffee and shelter," she suggested as we binned our wrappers. We set off at a slow jog, both of us wearing sandals and lightweight clothing. My jeans and little white top gave me no protection from the falling temperature. As we ran, faster now, along the harbour path a rising gust of wind whipped the new hat off her head and propelled it like a psychedelic flying saucer over the low wall and into the waters of the harbour.

Hurray, I thought, it's gone.

"Help, help, can you get my hat," she was shouting to a man on a boat below us. The rain pelted down soaking us to the skin.

"Leave it," I said. "He'll never get it back, look it's bobbing about now and must surely sink any second."

"I love it," she said.

"Hey, you there," I shouted to the man, "please can you get her hat back?" Quite clearly she really had lost her good sense when she saw that thing.

The man picked up a boathook and pulled the hat with ease towards his now rocking boat. He lifted it off the damaging sea water and held it up in the rain, waving it towards us. We were drenched, she began to laugh and blow him kisses. Oh please stop flirting with him I thought as I shivered, feeling the cold now the drama was over. He pointed to some metal steps running down the side of the harbour wall, indicating we should climb down them to get the hat, whilst he sheltered in his cabin doorway.

"No chance, oh no, not me," I squeaked when she looked imploringly at me. "Why can't he bring it up here?" I can't do heights.

She disappeared over the edge, forgetting her own fear she was off down the ladder before I had a chance to relent and go myself. I held my breath. What if she fell? I hoped I'd not have to go after her, heights made me dizzy. I couldn't bear it if she got hurt. I couldn't bear to watch, but I did. I won't say she's clumsy but she's not very agile these days, compared to me; I should have gone for her. I looked down those steps in terror, shivering with cold. She went very slowly and her knuckles were white from gripping the metal bars. Then I heard her shriek, and the water caught my attention, it had an awful muddy, murky look about it now. It was also choppy, causing all the little boats to bob about as if an electrical charge controlled their motion.

"Are you ok?" I called down to her.

"My foot slipped that's all, I'm fine, bumped my chin," she'd paused to collect herself. Fortunately no real harm was done; there wasn't a hat in the world worth taking a fall for and especially not an unpleasant one like this. I still wished I'd gone to get it for her and I resolved to always offer help straight away in future if she needed it. I felt so mean. She was safely at the bottom. The man had crossed from his boat over a couple more, and now stood on the one moored near the ladder. He helped her to step down on to the boat, holding her waist with both his hands. I watched in horror as she turned round and gave him a great big hug. What was she thinking hugging a strange man on a boat?

"You must let me thank you with a meal," she told him. I couldn't hear what else was said. They exchanged phone numbers whilst I froze on Bridlington's harbour side. First a new hat and now a new man, what next?

I was so relieved when Mum came back over the wall, carrying her wet hat. I loved her so very, very much. The rain had stopped and the wind eased up, the shower had just been a short sharp burst typical of this summer. I would always remember this day of happiness together no matter what our futures held. What would her hospital letter say? Had they found another problem in her recent scans?

I'd hardly ever seen my father, he lived too far away with his new family. We'd managed on our own and in my opinion we didn't need anyone else. But sometimes over the last year I had wished he'd been here to help us cope.

We hugged. "Today is my lucky day Jo, that man and me, we were good friends a long time ago. He's invited me out and I've said yes and I must thank my lucky hat for this chance encounter." We walked briskly towards the bus shelter dripping rain and sea water; Mum looked so happy and younger, despite being soaked to the skin. It was then I realised how hard it must have been for her to be alone all these years. I couldn't possibly begrudge her having a boyfriend even if I didn't have one any longer. Last week mine had dumped me for a girl I thought was a friend. I grew up a lot right then and realised just how lucky I was to have such a wonderful mum, although I'd never taken her for granted. We both had important letters to open when we got home and no matter what their contents were I knew we'd get through it together. My letter contained good news, I had a place at University, and Mum's was an appointment for a routine check-up in twelve months. At last our futures finally looked as bright as Mum's new

Skateboarding 50s Style
by Michael Perry

Seems we helped start a multi-million pound industry, with international competitions now commonplace. Our past-time enjoyment was the beginning of a new craze still in existence today. This in turn led on to Snowboarding, Windsurfing and Sand-boarding. Yes, a raft of new and exciting sports and several multi-million pound industries grew from our childhood pleasures.

Oh!...yes they did. It might not 'ave been as highly developed – or well known as nar – but we started it in the back streets of Leeds. Born at end of t'war, rationing still in existence and television still a dream for most, we had to amuse ourselves at weekends, holiday times, or after school.

Apart from t'usual football in t'streets, where we were constantly told, "Mind t'windows," or more often than not, "Get that mucky ball away frum our woshing," and "Go lake in't park." The park weren't too far off, but as many of us didn't have bikes, we'd 'ave 'ad to run on, or cadge a saddle from them wit bike.

Nar, don't git us wrong. Cause we's were fit then. 'Ad to be quick, specially as t'local bobby cum'd roond regular like. The's a few times hess near on 'ad us, climbing oot t'tusky field wi a reet gran stik in us 'ands. Eh! Wot yar mean? Yer no frum t'Morley triangle are yer. Tusky, well it luks like it, dunnit. Cept fer being green, but don't git that cos it gives yer t'belly-ache. But ifin it's ripe it's red, wi a reet big leaf on. A bit o' sugar from yer pocket lining, at'll sweeten it, an' it's best bit o' ru-bub thars 'ad.

Any 'ow, I were telling as 'ow we's fit like, an' we'd be running in t'park. After a bit, thems wi bikes ud leave us standing, we cudn't run all time. Nar some o' paths wer tarmac n sloped darn ta main gate. Onley gates 'ad gone, as 'ow them an' railings 'ad bin med into tanks fer feitting war wi Germany. Well best road fer us getting to tuck shop by park gate quick lik, wer on us skates.

Od on, yer say thims bin round fer years. Aye, I nos, but what we did wer to share wi us mates wat dint 'ave nun. Nar od on, cas 'ere's t'break thru' t'multi-million pund industry. We 'ad us Beano Annual, from Christmas, cept lasses ou 'ad Bunty or summint like it. An' thems all 'as copied us any 'ow. We'd put book on t'skate, sit on it an' belt down t'path to bottom t'ill. Odding on t'edge o' book we'd sway one road or t'uther t'steer, an' us 'eels on t'path to stop.

A few times we's 'ad us skin off t'knuckles, bur a bit o' spit an' a 'ankie we'd be reet. Best wer ginnel races. We'd go off an' mark out in chalk, (ifin teacher dint see us pinch a bit), a zig-zag course. An' using a few bricks from t'bomb sites wi a plank, or a bit o' tin roof, we'd build a tek-off ramp. Gangs o' us frum bottom side o' park, an' gangs frum topside o' park ud 'ave races down t'ginnel reglar. Then we'd run ta top o' ginnel, wi skate an' book, ready fer next run. I were fit then.

Now 'ere in Brid. they's just gotten a new skate park opened. Should 'ave got me an' me mates to open this 'ere new skate park. Well, we gor it all going. Them as med a load o' brass art o' this should 'av asked us; we'd mek summit out o' sport we started in t'1950s an' fer cost ov a bit o' chalk an' a few odd bricks.

An' we 'ad Lord Mayor oppen new park. Bur ar bet 'e can't beat me on t'Beano n skate. Eh, wot's a lad ta do 'ere ta git a race wit locals, or is they jist scared?

Oh I do like to be ...
by Les Penrose

A pleasant day at the seaside
A week at a B&B
Or maybe stay at a classy Hotel
Where they serve you afternoon tea
South-Shore, Sewerby, Flamborough Head
Old Town down to the Quay
Bingo, slot machines, fun of the fair
Plenty to do and to see
You could just sit taking in the view
Watching the world go by
A day or a week at the seaside
Raising your spirits high
The Harbour, the Spa
A walk down the prom
Maybe a splash in the sea
Ice-cream, candyfloss, sticks of rock
A pint - or more Yorkshire tea
There's Crazy Golf – beach-balls
Sand-castles – twelve holes
Burgers – fish – chips and peas
Or go down the Library – fiction or fact
Exploring your family tree
But you'd better watch out

For those ravenous gulls
They'll be after your fish & chips
Swooping in on a wing and a prayer
Snatching them from your lips
We've postcards to keep
Or send to friends
Mementoes of happy days out
Everything you could possibly want
And that's what it's all about.
You could sail round the bay
On the Yorkshire Belle
Perhaps in a pea-green boat
And there's no need to go
To far off lands where they
Say the bong-trees grow
Though we don't like to boast
We've got the lot - so
Please join me in a toast -
Come along - come and enjoy
It's all on the sunny East Coast
Roll-up, roll-up and give it a try
Just like your Granny once did
The visitors use its Sunday name
But the locals call it … Brid.

The Bridlington Lifeboat Men
by Joan Saxby

The lifeboat men risk their lives
To save the lives of others
Sailing through the raging seas
A proper band of brothers

The rise and fall of tidal waves
The panic of the drowning
They calmly ride the storm to save
Whoever, without frowning.

They don their oilskins to prepare
And never hesitate to think
Except for how they're going to care
For whom they rescue from the drink.

They do all this with little pay
For it's mostly voluntary
They'll go to rescue night or day
From danger they don't tarry.

It's not for food they man their boat
And risk the stormy wave
They confidently go afloat
For people's lives to save.

The Sentinel

White as the cliffs
Whereon it stands
White as the shells
On the shifting sands
Tall as the tales
That fishermen tell
Proudly erect
Above eddying swell
King of the headland
Majestic, serene,
Presence imposing
Surveying the scene
Light in the night
The seaman's guide
Beam crossing sea
Whatever the tide

Flash in the dark
Keeps ships on course
Silent the signal
Through elements' force
Boom of the foghorn warning of danger
"Keep away from the rocks both local and stranger."

by Audrey Bemrose

Bridlington - A Bird's Eye View
by Trev Haymer

Yesterday I had wings!

I've always harboured a secret passion for flying - not in our metal-tubed sardine tins, but to have my own set of wings and fly free as a bird over Bridlington and the farms and villages of East Yorkshire.

For my test flight I headed above the choked holiday traffic and jerky buses towards the seafront, a favourite place to have a coffee and listen to the gulls - my music of the seaside. What a wonderful feeling swooping over the forbidding yellow traffic lines, chortling at the traffic chaos below. Not for me, I thought...la, la, la. I have the freedom of the sky. Skimming through town I vaguely wondered if I needed a flying licence. Nearing the front my arms ached so I fluttered down and settled on the ledge of the former Woolworth building for a quick rest. Next to me was a row of seagulls, squawking and nodding to each other. They froze when I landed. Ten pairs of beady eyes silently swept over me. Then the nearest one squawked:

'Incomer?'

'Erm...I um...yes,' I replied shyly. 'But I live locally.'

The shiny eyes and curved orange beak stared at me.

'Ah, hence the Bridlington Town scarf and flying boots?'

'Erm...yes...erm, must be what I came out in,' I stammered.

'Ah well,' Yorkie squawked, 'yer'll be all right here. This ledge is fer incomers, mainly from them inland council tips. All the locals are on t'harbour front, fighting them fat pigeons fer chips.'

A small gull wearing an iod piped up. 'Except me, old love.'

'Oh yeah, forgot you, Doris,' the gull squawked, turning back to me. 'She's learning Albanian in case we get invaded soon.' A sound like a chuckle. 'Anyroad, I'll introduce you to me mates. I'm Yorkie an' this lad next ter me is Scottie - bit of a lad Scottie is.

I shot Scottie a quick glance. I could smell beer fumes emanating from him. He was wearing a stained sporran and swaying alarmingly on the lip of the ledge.

'Aye,' Yorkie continued. 'Scottie's got an ASBO on him. He wer out last weekend swiggin' leftovers in a beer garden.'

'Oh,' I said, 'was he drunk?'

'I'll say. But he finished the night off peckin' at a curry carton fer his supper, slipped in a puddle of ice cream, got trodden on an' ended up fightin' mad down t'harbour front.'

I smiled uneasily then blurted, 'Oh dear. Well, best be off.'

Yorkie locked his wing onto mine. 'Mind you - Scottie's done it before, y'know.' His squawk sounded like a titter. 'The poor lad's been swept up twice. Absolutely blotto he gets, but he loves ice cream as well as beer.'

I tried to pull away but his grip tightened. Yorkie shuffled his pale-orange webbed feet. 'Must tell yer this - Scottie'd had a few once. He were swoopin' down ter get a little lad's fish an' chips but misjudged it an' landed in t'lad's mother's hair! A right tangle it were, chips an' white feathers everywhere.' He paused for breath. 'The lad's mother yelled, 'Yer feathered freak - I've just been to the soddin' hairdressers!' She clouted Scottie with her handbag.' He glared at Scottie. 'Yer dumb haggis - yer shouldn't drink when yer flying.'

'Duh...I know that yer numb Yorkshire pudding.'

I winced at the insults. 'Well I really must be...'

'No, no,' Yorkie objected. 'Yer haven't met Dolly yet.' He pointed along the row to a pretty young seagull. 'That lass is Dolly. Been preenin' herself all morning. She'll be off out ter night in her red Jimmy Choo shoes an' blue Coco Chanel skirt. She's a looker don't yer think?'

'Tart,' Scottie squawked.

Yorkie ignored him. 'Dolly has her tail feathers permed once a month - says it makes her legs look slimmer. And she's obsessed with cleanliness, she is. See the back-pack she's wearin'? It's baby-wipes from that Pound shop. Good on her, I say.' He burped. 'Us gulls 'ave a bad enough name as it is.'

'Yes she's quite a bird,' I murmured, shaking my wings. 'Ah well, I'd best get some flying practice in.'

Yorkie sighed wistfully. 'Dolly will be puttin' her lippy on any minute now.' He turned to me. 'Yer clip-on wings are a bit squeaky, lad...tha needs a drop of WD40 on 'em.'

'Oh. Okay I'll fix them. Well...see you guys later.'

Yorkie wouldn't release me. 'Last year Dolly went down ter that London, y'know.'

'Slapper,' Scottie squawked.

Yorkie gave him a nasty peck. 'Dolly went 'cos she gets bored up here. Aye, she met this geezer mincin' along t'Embankment. He were a bit 'up himself', she told me. He'd dyed his tail feathers blue an' pink and he squawked with a lisp -said he were a Talent Agent.'

I nodded. 'Well, I really must be…'

'Yeah,' Scottie interrupted. 'The wee lassie wanted to go on that X Factor thing.'

'Hey - keep yer beak out yer Scottish layabout,' Yorkie bristled. 'I'm tellin' t'tale.'

Yorkie turned back to me. 'Yeah well, Dolly heard that Cowell fella likes girls.'

I gazed anxiously at the weakening sun and impatiently rattled my squeaky wings. Yorkie gave me a disapproving look.

'Anyroad,' he squawked. 'This agent got Dolly on t'show. But Cowell didn't like her squawkin' an' dancin' routine - her orange webs tapping all over t'stage.' A sound like a chuckle. 'And he certainly didn't like the gooey mess on the stage when Dolly got excited.'

'She was never sick on the stage?' I gasped in horror.

'Oh no...it wer t'other end! All green an' white…'

'And it didna help when the wee lassie fell off the stage onto the judges' table,' Scottie interrupted.

Yorkie nodded. 'Yeah. She'd scoffed a tub of rum and raisin ice cream backstage for her nerves.'

'Oh dear, what a shame,' I mumbled.

Yorkie squawked with glee. 'Having failed, she got her own back. She flew up on top of Cowell's head and dropped one of her Sunday specials!' A squawky titter rippled along the ledge.

Bunch of nutters, I thought. I pointedly stared at my watch. 'Well it's been nice…'

A sudden flurry of wings. An elderly gull was grabbed as he nearly tottered off the ledge. 'Nay, Walter lad,' Yorkie panted to me. 'Poor old lad's wings keep seizing up.' He sniffed then gazed down at the mess on Walter's orange-webbed foot. 'What HAVE yer done, old lad?' he chastised. He sighed heavily. 'Yer going in a Home you are.'

Grinning weakly I rustled my wings. Got to get away from this lot before they get me as daft as they are. I struggled loose as two RAF jets screamed across the sky. 'Toodle pip, then,' I shouted. Yorkie grabbed me, clamping his wing to mine again. He pointed to the end of the row where a fat gull sat preening.

'Nay lad, stay. Yer've not met Bomber yet. His flying skills are legendary.' Yorkie's curved beak pointed at the infamous high rise flats overlooking the harbour. 'See that carbuncle?'

I nodded and growled, 'That eyesore. How the Council Planning dumbos came to pass that I'll never know.'

Yorkie's eyes flashed. 'Aye, but from the top of them flats there's a great view of the invisible Marina! He, he.'

'No, I were going ter say,' he continued. 'Last Bank Holiday, Bomber takes off from the top of them flats, he swoops down across the harbour, then, passing under the bridge, he executes three high-speed twirls. Shooting out t'other side, he performs two figure eights across the car park then lands doing an army roll. He just misses a coach load of pensioners.'

Much squawking.

'But when Bomber sees all them pensioners he gets up, does a bombing run across the harbour an' releases his Dambuster! A woman with a Zimmer frame cops it first, then a man in a wheelchair, trying to avoid it he cannons in ter them railings, his fish an'chips went flying all over t'place.'

I shot Yorkie a sickly smile.

'Oh, but Bomber's very fair. He lets out two deafening squawks as a warning, giving 'em time to take cover. See, them pensioners don't move so fast.'

I struggled, but Yorkie was stronger than he looked. His wing remained firmly clamped to mine. He nodded his head. 'Now Bomber's practising a Dambusters' run along Promenade - can't wait.'

'Och aye,' Scottie put in gleefully. 'He wants to catch all them holidaymakers when they come out of the bingo.' He appeared to grin wickedly. 'But the wee laddie needs to feed up on thick grain for that.' I shuddered at the thought.

Yorkie was gazing down at the bustling street below. 'Hey Bomber,' he said suddenly. 'Traffic Warden alert!' He pointed his beak. 'Look, one of them hated wardens is about to ticket that family car. It belongs to visitors, kids an' all. I saw 'em arrive about an hour ago.'

'Welcome to Bridlington,' I murmured.

Bomber waddled along the ledge. 'I see him.'

'Quick!' Yorkie squawked. 'He's taking his cap off ter scratch his head before slapping a ticket on their car. Go-Go-Go!' Bomber zoomed low across the crowded street.

'Splat!'

'He, he he. One hundred an' eighty!' Yorkie squawked, doing a little jig. The other gulls applauded the bullseye by flapping furiously.

I smiled. 'Well done, erm...Bomber. Over-zealous traffic wardens - it puts visitors off coming to our town and its lovely beaches.'

'Well,' Scottie yawned, 'Best be away...early night. I've to be up at the crack of dawn - lots of chimneys to perch on and squawk down.'

It crossed my mind it would be getting dark soon and I'd no navigation lights. Yorkie loosened his grip to preen so I swiftly took off. I banked around the twin piers and harbour then up to Jeromes. My throat felt parched so I ordered a strawberry ice cream. I received some funny looks. Then I decided to head for the Priory Church at Bridlington's Old Town. I passed the yellow speedboat klaxoning its way across the bay. White-faced passengers were clinging on for dear life.

Arriving at the Priory Church I perched on a spire as my arms were tiring. Up here the air was tangy with salt and the waft of fish and chips kept teasing my nostrils. The view was breathtaking. I spotted the Pirate boat crossing the bay. Flag-waving children whooping as they rolled along 'white horses'. This was more like it - well away from those dratted seagulls.

Turning, I watched visitors, slurping coloured ice creams, thronging the streets of Old Town. Narrowing my eyes against the wind I saw a white speck approaching. 'Oh no,' I groaned, 'I can't cope with another seagull!'

A rustling of wings behind me. Yorkie was perched there wearing an oafish grin. 'Ee by gum lad,' he squawked. 'Yer don't wanna be perchin' here.'

I shot him a sickly grin. 'Why are you here?'

'Yer never said terrah properly did yer?' He scanned the sky. Streaks of orange and pink lay across the horizon. 'Yeah,' Yorkie squawked, 'we don't perch up 'ere 'cos of them hawks. They'll come sweeping down like Red Arrers an' have yer leg off afore yer can say - Flamborough Head. Anyway, did I tell you...'

I groaned. Here we go again. I had a sudden flash of inspiration. 'HAWKS,' I yelled.

Yorkie hurtled back towards the seafront.

I flew home thinking I might nip over to Scarborough tomorrow if my arms feel up to it. Perch on the front and treat myself to a Knickerbocker Glory and.... A draught from the open window pimpled my bare arms. I got off my bed to close it and trod on something soft. My Bridlington Town scarf lay discarded like some kind of python. My brown, fur-lined builders' boots stood awry at the foot of the bed. The wardrobe door was half open - I caught a glimpse of something white and feathery hanging there. The bedroom floor was strewn with feathers. Puzzled, I glanced down at my pyjamas. They were smeared with strawberry ice cream stains.

The Return
by Julia Oldham

It was the day after my marriage when I arrived at my new home high in the northern hills. Driving through the smoke-veiled towns with their grimy mills now contrasted sharply against the stone-walled lush green fields which rose to the heathered moors of the Pennines. This welcome breath of clean air filled my lungs and made my heart throb so much that, when I returned to live in Yorkshire this year, the same sensation hit me. I had come back to a county that had been my home for twenty-six years before emigrating to Spain. Let it be known
that I was a "comer in" all those years ago, but now, I think you could say for certain, I am here to stay.

    My lungs fill with the aroma of freshly caught fish as I lean over the harbourside where the boats are unloading their daily catch of fish, lobsters and crabs which will be eaten in the now not so grimy towns full of exotic eateries. I walk along the quayside smelling fish and chips, waffles and the forever popular dishes of mussels and prepared crab, reminding me of the holidays with my sons, who would always succumb to an ice cream whilst watching the mud boat and the Flamborian go out on an excursion. Even the speedboat is still making those rapid trips out to sea, but now the passengers include my grandchildren.

    I cannot think of any visit to this staid Yorkshire town that was displeasing; even our dog enjoyed running on the windswept beaches in winter and paddling in the clear cold sea.

In Praise Of Bridlington
by Anne Mullender

Magical childhood memories
stay with me still today.
Round the corner of Kingston Road
spreads the view of Bridlington Bay.

Excitement courses through me
for here I am at last.
'Can you smell the briny sea, dear?'
Mother's voice echoes from the past.

Never in my wildest dreams
did it occur to me
one day I should come to live here
in Bridlington by the sea.

Warm, welcoming, and friendly
The Spa hosts splendid shows.
By the Harbour I stop to pat
Mr Nicholls' 'Henry' on the nose.

Pop into the Library, Bank,
have coffee at Chapel Street
wander through The Promenades
who knows whom I'm going to meet?

I visit Boots or M & S
Up busy King Street I roam
I walk through this friendly town
That I'm happy to call my home.

All Hallows Eve
by Patricia Susan Dixon MacArthur

Walking by the Priory
on All Hallows Eve
I teetered past the gravestones
in my highest heels
The night was black, wisps of cloud
cloaked a watery moon
Behind me something groaned out loud,
as streetlights dimmed right down
Turning round I saw a ghost
garbed in a sheet of white
Holding hands with a werewolf
his sharp teeth shone so bright
When bats flew from the belfry
the clock then struck thirteen
Frankenstein and Dracula
out enjoying the night scene
Said please don't worry darlin'
you have nothing to fear
From the spooks of Bridlington
on this night of the year
They're simply exercising
the right they have to roam
So at that very moment
I ran all the way home
Shoes in hand and broomstick too
I was the little witch that flew.

Sewerby Village
by Wendy Harrison

The village of Sewerby is approximately one and a half miles out of Bridlington and currently, in 2013, has 160 properties, many of them now holiday lets.

Sewerby is considered to be the jewel in the crown of the East Riding of Yorkshire and, without mentioning the magnificent Sewerby Hall and Gardens, which is well documented throughout the ages, the village of Sewerby has an appeal of its own.

We share our beautiful area with many visitors, who come all the year round and enjoy this scenic part of Bridlington. Not only does Sewerby offer serene scenery of white cliffs looking towards Flamborough, but interesting views of Bridlington with the sea crashing against the harbour wall on a stormy day, and on a calm day, a flat calm sea that looks as if one could walk across the water to Bridlington.

Walking groups hold regular meetings and walk to Danes Dyke. This is only a short walk by the cliffs or the beach, and takes one through the Links golf course. On reaching Danes Dyke there is a tree trail through the woodlands with carved leaf markers, showing the names of the trees around. Occasionally you will meet one of the tent dwellers who inhabit a copse. Winter and summer they exist happily, or unhappily, one never knows. They do no harm to anyone and always have a friendly word when spoken to.

Most of the cottages in the conservation area of Main Street were built for the workers from the Sewerby Hall estate, some of which are Grade II listed and date from the 1600s. However, most of the terraced cottages were built in the 1700s.

Sewerby Hall and Gardens (Grade I listed) is a magnificent place to visit. With manicured parkland and walled gardens, a zoo, café, and of course the house itself; this is currently undergoing renovations, restoring the house to its original state in the 1900s.

There are two churches in Sewerby. The Wesleyan Methodist Chapel was built in 1962; the original chapel, built in 1825 is now a commemorative garden, and prior to that a barn was licensed for worship in 1800 followed by a house in 1818. George Gilbert Scott (later to be known as Sir Gilbert Scott) designed St. John the Evangelist's Church (Grade II Listed) which was completed in 1848. These two churches – one at each end of the village – are well supported and hold many functions throughout the week.

Sewerby is extremely fortunate to be able to boast three buildings, all having been designed by the world-famous architect, Sir Gilbert Scott; among other designs credited to him are the Albert Memorial and St Pancras Hotel, both in London.

Next to the entrance of Sewerby Hall, stands what was once the village school. The school (Grade II listed) was designed by Sir Gilbert Scott in 1849 in the Gothic style. It closed in 1949 and was converted to a private residence by Francis Johnson, a leading Bridlington architect.

Entering the village from Bridlington, there is a splendid Grade II listed building, Sewerby Grange, which was built as a Vicarage in the late 1800s. It is now a licensed hotel. This Gothic style building was also designed by Sir Gilbert Scott.

It is quite something for such a small village to have so many businesses. Nestled amongst the Grade II listed cottages in Main Street, there is a hairdresser, a caravan site, a fish shop and a restaurant/tearoom. At the end of Cliff Road there is the 'Bondville Model Village', which also has a tearoom; no excuse to go hungry or thirsty in Sewerby.

Sewerby's local alehouse, 'The Ship Inn' on Cliff Road, is built in the late Georgian style. Enclosure maps of 1802 and 1811 show an Inn on the same site and in 1823 it was listed as an alehouse called the 'Bottle and Glass'.

Sewerby Cricket Club is situated in front of Sewerby Hall on the cliff-top with the stunning backdrop of Bridlington Bay. This is a cricket club to be proud of. Officially formed in 1879 and winning many cups along the way, it is a pleasure to sit and watch the game during the season. Refreshments can be bought from the rear of the pavilion, where the ladies of the club make cups of tea and coffee, along with gorgeous home-made cakes and bacon sandwiches, which can be bought by spectators or passers-by. The local history book 'The Village of Sewerby Then & Now' has an interesting article about the history of the cricket club by one of its late members, Mr. Carl Robinson. This can be found in the local history section in either one of the two Libraries in Bridlington.

Apart from people visiting the area, migrating birds can be seen on their way to warmer climates. In October this year, hiding behind a small conifer bush, was a little bird, looking very much like a blackbird in size and colour, yet having a wide fawn bib on its chest. I emailed the RSPB at Bempton, and they informed me that it was a female ringed ouzel; the male bird has a white bib. They went on to say that I was very privileged to see such a bird as they are very private. If it hadn't been for my nosy Cocker Spaniel called Harvey, I would never have looked behind the bush. It later flew away to resume its long journey to southern Spain.

Sewerby is very different to the excitement and thrills of the centre of Bridlington. In contrast, Sewerby offers peace, tranquility and outdoor interests for all ages.

**Winter's Tune
by Trev Haymer**

Night;
Dark skeletons of shivering trees
Prod a raging sky. They howl for the spiky
Comfort of a black crow's nest – yearn for
the rustling warmth of the green gown of Spring –
Weep for the errant swallow's return.

Dawn;
In the curved arm of Brid's long bay,
Blue-arsed sheep paddle in white fields.
They gnaw in the tired blink of a proud lighthouse,
Phallic sentry of the night whose glassy nipples
Crown milky cliffs slashed by the orange beaks of puffins.

Day;
A thin dog crabs the shell-dusted beach,
Sniffing at worm-curled sand –
Waves a bent leg at the incoming tide –
Leaves a bark and its own high-water mark.

Tomorrow;
No swimmer's hand will daub
Winter's mackerel sky straddling this shy town.
The land will sigh – squeezed by a wet sea fret –
Dark shags will dip – cormorants sip,
While winter warbles her harsh tune.

A Surprise Caller
by Michael Perry

I'd just taken the refilled teapot into the conservatory as the doorbell rang that Sunday morning after breakfast. As my wife had just finished clearing the breakfast things in the kitchen and was nearest, she answered the call. The young lady, holding a closed briefcase clutched across her breast, asked if this was the home of a Mr Michael Longton and if so could she talk to him. As I'd heard my name, I walked to the door and said, "Yes that's me. How can I help you?" The young lady looked at me then my wife, and with a nervous voice said, "It may be embarrassing but I think you are my father."

My wife Elaine looked at me with raised eyebrows and tight lips, holding back the obvious questions. "I've some things here to help explain why I believe I'm your daughter," she said, as she held the briefcase forward.

"You'd best come in and explain," I said stepping back and holding the door open. Elaine led the way to the conservatory, and gesturing to a chair invited her to sit. We sat opposite her, waiting for her nerves to settle, my wife pouring tea for us all.

"I'm Susan Tomlinson, seventeen and living in Newcastle. I've just had my school exam results and have been awarded a college place for next year." She started pulling papers from her case, backing up her spoken word. Elaine and I had been married for twenty years now and had a family. Elaine's furrowed brow and piercing eyes burrowed into mine.

"How did you get my name and address here in Bridlington? And what makes you think I'm possibly your father?" I asked.

"You were a sales representative when you knew my mother, and stayed in Newcastle several times and saw her there before I was born back in 1985. But then you and mother went separate ways and we moved to Sunderland as mum took up a career there."

"What's your mother's name?" asked Elaine.

"She was June Susan Tomlinson," replied Susan, holding forth a small collection of photographs. We took these and as I gazed at them could see the likeness of mother and daughter. I also recalled the warm smiling face of June just as my memories of her had remained from all those years ago. Sat at the side of me I couldn't make out Elaine's expression as she had turned slightly away from me, but I knew she was choking up inside. Her body had stiffened and her grip on the photographs had tightened as she stared at them and back to Susan.

"Was?" I said. "You said your mother was June Tomlinson. Has she married or changed her name?"

"No, I...I wish that were possible." A long silence followed as Susan with eyes filling and head bent bit her bottom lip. "She died in May, just after I'd finished my exams. It was while I was clearing out her wardrobe I came across a box with all these things in which led me to you." There in her hand was a large photo of June with me embracing her and the look of love in both of us. "Oh, it's not what you may think. Mother provided well for me, she'd taken out insurance which will pay for my education and the house is now paid for, so I'm not here to expect you to support me or anything."

Elaine quickly rose from her seat and dropping the photos hurried to the kitchen, where we heard her weeping and then blow her nose several times, while her sobbing continued.

"Well we'd better introduce you to your half brothers and sisters," I said. "They'll be home from morning prayers soon. You'll be a big surprise for them."

"I've been an only one and never thought of brothers or sisters. How many sisters have I?" she asked in excited tone.

"Eleven," said Elaine walking in from the kitchen holding a tissue in one hand to red watery eyes.

"Eleven brothers and sisters?" repeated Susan.

"No eleven sisters," Elaine corrected, "and nine brothers." Susan stopped smiling as her eyes widened and jaw dropped slightly trying to comprehend the fact that now she had twenty half siblings.

"And you don't mind?" she said to Elaine.

"Not at all, I hope you'll think of me as your second mother. The other mothers will take to you too."

"Other mothers?"

"There are seven of us in this family and three husbands too. But we Mormons always have larger families."

Oh Little Town Of Bridlington
by Joan Saxby

Oh little town of Bridlington
How lucky that you are
To have a brand new harbour
And a brand new Spa.

Oh little town of Bridlington
You can shout out loud
That you're soon to have a harbour
Of which you can be proud.

Oh little town of Bridlington
You're designed to be the host
To many happy tourists
On the North East Yorkshire coast.

Oh little town of Bridlington
Our treasure on the East
It's far too long you've waited
But now you should be pleased.

Oh little town of Bridlington
So proud you'll be that's sure
When all the rich and famous
Come visiting your door.

Oh little town of Bridlington
Be happy that it's you
When all the ships come sailing in
And make your vision true.

Audrey Bemrose

I've always loved words and could already read before I started Lissett Village School. At Bridlington High School I was able to study Latin, French and German and still enjoy checking derivations when solving crosswords. Over 30 years ago I took part in the National Federation of Women's Institutes 'Scene 80' involving writing, acting, local history, folk-lore etc. I performed some of my East Riding Dialect poems in the old Driffield Town Hall, then went on to the North East Regional Festival at the People's Theatre, Newcastle. The final presentation was at the Shakespeare Memorial Theatre at Stratford, but I was only in the audience for that one. Next I joined the former Heritage Poets, then in 1988 became a founder member of the Bridlington Writers' Group. We still meet weekly. Both groups have entertained numerous organisations locally. One of the trio which won the first writing contest held after the Bridlington Library Writers began in 2011, I have also had some successes in Yorkshire area competitions. Besides dialect, I enjoy writing humour, reminiscence, and sometimes more serious subjects, as well as researching and family history

Mark Cunningham

I was born in Doncaster and moved to Bridlington in 2010. I work at Sewerby Hall and Gardens and at Flamborough Lighthouse.

I started writing poems then having my young daughter gave me the idea to write short stories for young children.

In June 2013 Lodge books published this my first book.

I have more story books in the pipeline and these too will be published by Lodge Books.

THE DOVE TALE

Mark Cunningham

Michaela Goodale-Truelove

I have lived in Bridlington since the age of three and for me the town's greatest asset is its geography: a truly inspirational place for the writer or artist. As a child I would escape to the Wendy house at the bottom of the garden where I could read, draw or write undisturbed. My school days were certainly not the happiest days of my life and I left at seventeen disillusioned, but enrolling on an Art course proved to be a landmark decision, which led me to pass A-level Art and to study Graphic Design at Scarborough Tech before gaining my degree at Hull. Music also plays a significant role in my life; I am a founding member and vocalist of rock band Alice in Thunderland.

I joined the Bridlington Library Writers' Group purely by chance, after attending a talk given by the remarkable children's author Christina M. Butler, and I have found our monthly meetings both delightful and informative.
I live with my beloved husband in a home filled with books, pictures, records and favourite possessions.

David Hawkins

Writing is something I have always enjoyed doing, even in my schooldays.

On retirement in 1997 I joined a writing class and attended lectures by professional writers in order to improve my technique. I have written short stories and poetry, some of which have been printed in booklet form: Out of Rhyme; Just in Rhyme; Shorelines and Seasons; Along the Shoreline; and It's Not Cricket.

An Old Boy of my Senior School was Surgeon Captain Edward Leicester Atkinson who went with Captain Scott's British Antarctic Expedition in 1910, prompting me to write 'The Man Who Found Captain Scott' for the school's celebration of the expedition's centenary in 2012. A copy of the booklet is now in a dedicated room for Atkinson memorabilia at the school.

Wendy Harrison

I was born and bred in Hull and worked for Hull Corporation Telephones in the accounts dept. I subsequently lived and worked in Leeds for 40 years and became an active member of a local dramatic society, the 'Scholes Village Players'.
On retiring in 2000 we moved back to East Yorkshire, where I decided that my hobby needed to change. Reg and I were encouraged to join the Sewerby Village Residents Association and the Bridlington & District Civic Society and we enjoy being a part of both. My writing began with writing the Bridlington & District Civic Society newsletter for the Bridlington Free Press and, along with Marilyn Berrigan, I wrote, edited and produced the local history book 'Sewerby Village Then & Now', which can be found in both libraries.
My interest in writing continues to grow, and encouragement from the writers' group at our monthly meetings is very much appreciated.
Bridlington is a very artistic place to live. We have such beautiful scenery, which in turn gives one the enthusiasm for art, music, and drama.

Trev Haymer

Trev Haymer lives in Bridlington with his wife Lorraine (Little Boss). He has 4 daughters who have stumbled from the nest, 8 grandchildren and 8 gt grandchildren. Likes: Art, Literature, Bob Dylan, Blues singers and Footy. Trev has published: Poetry—'Diamond Lil and other Gems'; and, 'Inside Trevor's Shorts' (short stories). Both are available at Lodge Books, South Back Lane, Bridlington.

Lesley Ince

I'm a Southerner who moved here eight years ago and was given a warm Yorkshire welcome by the Bridlington Writers' Group. Writing has always been an important part of my life.

The Bridlington Library Writer's Group, of which I'm proud to be a member, has also been very inspiring and supportive.

Ken Joul

Kenneth Joul is also the author of the novel *Legacy of the Ancients*, available from Lodge Books or Amazon. After a working life of preparing reports and minutes for a Metropolitan Local Authority, he decided after retirement to continue to work with words and write the novel.

Since joining the Bridlington Library Writers' Group, he has been enthused to write a follow up novel; so keep looking out for it. He has also carried out voluntary work as a Group Scout Leader; Secretary to the Management Committee of a local village hall; and Treasurer of a branch of Arthritis Care, which has now disbanded through lack of membership. He also has his emerald badge for being a blood donor. He has been married for 47 years and has three children and two grandchildren.

Sue MacArthur

Patricia Susan Dixon MacArthur was born and lives in Bridlington. A part-time freelance writer since 2005, she has had over 100 poems published: Poetic Images, 2006 a collection of previously published poems. She is also the author of Not a Guide to Bridlington, published in 2013.

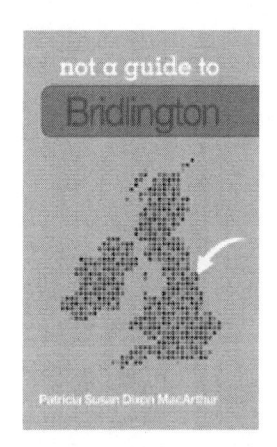

Anne Mullender

Born on Christmas Day, 1939 at Otley, West Yorkshire, Anne had no intention of choosing the Poetry Module in the National Extension College Correspondence Course for Creative Writing. However in 1996, she not only attempted this module, but she was hooked on poetry. Anne published her collection of poems, *Spreading My Wings,* in January 2011.
Anne became a member of Bridlington Writers' Group and was Secretary for 9 years. During this time her poetry and short stories were widely published in the small press, *Psychopoetica, Reach, Acorn, Linkway, Hilton House, Forward Press, Quantum Leap.* Recent successes include a Highly Commended for her poem, *February Third, 2009,* and a Certificate of Commendation for her poem, *One Bonfire Night.*
For two and a half years, Anne introduced members of Bridlington U3A to Creative Writing, encouraging new writers to explore the different genres. Currently, Anne is a member of Bridlington Library Writers' Group and enjoying being part of a vibrant band of men and women who are keen to publish their work, whilst forming new friendships and meeting established authors.

Julia Oldham

Julia was an enthusiastic writer in her childhood and also contributed to magazines and newspapers in her working life. She spent many years in Yorkshire before emigrating to Spain, and her return to the county this year re-ignited her passion for writing, which is reflected in her contributions to this anthology of Bridlington. She is also the author of *Camel Humps and Strawberries*, a 'warts and all' true adventure of emigrating to Spain; this is available only through Lodge Books.

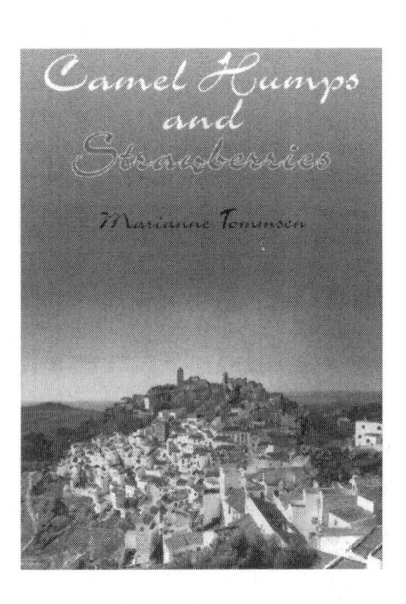

Michael Perry

Born in Suffolk, Michael spent his school years in Leeds and his early working life in West Yorkshire.

Following twenty years as a company representative Michael settled as a sub-Postmaster as his fitness to drive, cause by a spinal complaint, worsened. He finally retired back to the Yorkshire seaside town of Bridlington, a place of many a happy childhood holiday.

A typical Yorkshire humour, born from the observations of years of serving the public, can be seen in much of his writing,

Les Penrose

Les has been an active member of the Bridlington Library Writers' Group for approaching two years now. He enjoys writing poetry and short stories.

Joan Saxby

I was born in Yorkshire but spent the largest part of my life in Worksop, Nottinghamshire. Now I live back in Yorkshire on the beautiful east coast in Bridlington. I am a retired medical secretary and later secretary in industry. My hobbies are art and poetry writing. My art includes: oil painting landscapes, seascapes and animals; watercolour painting flowers and landscapes; pastel painting landscapes and flowers; and some ink work. I am working towards publishing a book of children's poems.

Also published by Lodge Books

Lost and Found
Andy Brown

Sugar to Rice
Andy Brown

Equally Insignificant
Andy Hutchinson

The Moon Via Scotch Corner
Andy Hutchinson

The Last Ramone Standing
Andy Hutchinson

See A Side of Bridlington
Bridlington Library Writers

For Just This Once!
Les Poetaster

Unabridged Rivers of my Mind
Les Poetaster

The Dove Tale
Mark Cunningham

Time Capsule
Peter Thompson

First Yacht Home
Peter Thompson

The Guy Fawkes Agenda
Peter Thompson

Diamond 'Lil and other Gems
Trev Haymer

Lost Lives
Val Creasey

A Far Reaching Dream
Andrew Milner

Raju, The Last Bear That Danced
Caron Gaske

101